MW01114320

EXPECT SUNSHINE

EXPECT SUNSHINE

A NOVEL BY

BETTY L. BUSH

A Tribute to the African-American Farmer

Museum Charity Publishing
Atlanta, Georgia

Publisher's Cataloging-in-Publication
    (Provided by Quality Books, Inc)

Bush, Betty L.
    Expect sunshine : a tribute to the
    African-American farmer : a novel / by Betty L.
    Bush -- 1st ed.
       p. cm.
       LCCN: 00-132112
       ISBN: 0-9679646-2-8

       1. Afro-American farmers--Georgia--Fiction.
    2. Agriculture--Georgia--Fiction.   I. Title.

    PS3552.U84E97 2000   813.6
                          QBI00-332

Published by
Museum Charity Publishing
P. O. Box 90698
Atlanta, Georgia 30364

To my father Charlie O. Bush Sr. who farms, loving and enjoying fully life in His Majesty

A most special dedication and tribute to the
African-American farmer who were 900,000 strong at the
turn of the twentieth century and on the eve of the
twenty-first century are fewer than 18,000

CHAPTER ONE

*E*llie stood at a bare window with her back to Kent in their secret meeting place, an old abandoned barn. The rusty tin roof shelter sat in a thicket of tall Georgia pine trees between their houses. On the boundary of two properties, it had been their undiscoverable hiding place, as children growing up on adjacent farms, and later as teenage lovers until she disappeared for twenty years.

The only true witness to their forever-bonded souls had aged well in spite of losing its window hinges and shutters in the midst of faithful summer hurricanes. Made of wood logged by Kent's grandfather two generations ago, the barn had been a corral for lazy horses and a stockade for bundles of freshly harvested hay. It had already been abandoned and forgotten before it became a refuge for the long ago lovers, Ellie and Kent.

Six months ago, Ellie unwillingly moved from

Chicago back to Chester. She had come to the peaceful sanctuary to purge her heartaches about returning and to meet her estranged companion.

On this Sunday evening, the near dusk hour barely lifted the parching summer heat, which was pounding the metal top above their heads. Kent had planted his tall brown walnut body in the center of the barn and was leaning against a single wooden post. He stood wide-legged wearing a plaid cotton shirt and blue jeans frazzled from his high-top field boots. His tightly curled hair was dusty from feeding the cattle before supper. He smelled faintly of lavender fading away from her oozing pores.

She remained quiet at the window, picturing them as they were twenty years ago, when she was his bride-to-be. As carefree teenagers they had been in love. Now, the pilgrimage here was different. So long apart, Ellie remembered the last time Kent's strong arms caressed her and relished the moment. After taking one deep breath of desire, she disturbed the vivid memory and lost it as easily as it came. Ellie wondered if the man she left twenty years earlier ever recalled the warm and wonderful past together that she could not seem to put aside.

Pink streaks of early dusk splashed against the summer sky in front of Ellie, illuminating her thin body. She was more beautiful than Kent remembered tall and shapely with a head full of hair in wild, short natural ringlets. Her brown eyes and smooth teak-colored skin were like tempered caramels. She wore a yellow sleeveless tank with a white tee shirt underneath and two pocket khakis.

8

From where Kent rested, he viewed the field's thick brown grass and the distant green treetops through the missing huge double barn doors to the right of her. The silence made him uncomfortable, and he tried his best to think of anything but his lasting love for Ellie. After she left, he continued to farm while dreaming of her returning to him. Kent never gave up hope that Ellie would one day come back. When her face was becoming a faded memory, she shocked him and all of Chester by reappearing to live next door as the adjacent farmer's wife.

Kent fanned a stubborn horsefly as he waited for Ellie to turn around. He repeatedly kicked small pieces of dried brittle straw to keep his mind in the right place. Smashing the lifeless hay to dust, it practically disappeared into the dirt. Standing there, the stacked and scattered hay reminded Kent of feeding his last horse named Smokey.

He leaned heavier on the post that supported the stall where the old mare once lived. A school of large square nails were hammered near the top and bottom of the post. He put his hands on the solid beam behind him and rubbed the top nail heads, recalling the vicious weather that wounded Smokey.

In the tender years of Kent's youth, the huge black mare, frightened in a summer storm, fell down sideways in her stall. Caught underneath the bottom panel, her neck beat with the rough wind's tempo on the stall until she broke it trying to hide from the flashing lightning and loud thunder.

Lost in the sorrowful memory, Kent did not see Ellie turn around to watch him with lustful eyes taking in every delicate detail. She loved the man across from her, whom circumstances and mostly her choices had made untouchable. Her secrets of the past rained heavily against their ever being together. Not a day passed by back in Chester that Ellie had not hoped for Kent's love to set her free from her mistakes.

✳✳✳

In the barn twenty years ago in nearly the same spot, Kent had proposed marriage to his only love, Ellie. She had said yes, and dreamed of the soon-to-come days as husband and wife. They were so much in love. But three days before their wedding, Ellie stood here with Kent shaking in despair, saying her last wish was to be a farmer's wife. She would leave on the next train to Chicago.

That moment was etched into his memory like thick grooves in a large oak tree, unlikely to ever wear away. Kent stared past Ellie through the open windowless space of the barn behind her. A purple hue had nudged the pink sky aside, signaling that the sun would soon sleep. In his mind he could still hear Ellie speaking the dreadful words, which had changed their lives.

Back then, her voice came from an empty place in a person he hardly recognized, "I love you Kent. You know it, but I have to leave this place."

Her words hung in the air.

"You'll never leave your father or this land."

She tapped her chest and said, "I must go or I'll regret it." Then searching for words to validate her abrupt decision, she broke his heart saying, "I'm afraid I'll hate you if you ask me to stay."

Terror propelled her words, but she stated them strongly. Her mind was made up; it was unshakable.

In tears, Ellie searched for his eyes then, as she was doing now. With her hands out-stretched trembling still hiding her secrets of the past, Ellie waited. Kent did nothing. She watched him watching her, and the horrible truth began to sink in—they must now live separate lives.

After all these years, Kent was still devastated by Ellie's sudden decision to leave him. His sad long-lashed eyes said it all. She knew without a doubt in her heart that he would not hold her, because he could not. For the first time since being back in Chester, Ellie realized that her return was harder on him.

Twenty years ago, Kent had torn out of the barn without a word, as she sobbed. Tears fell on Ellie's new princess crushed-laced white wedding dress. For that special day, she had chosen one with an empire waist that had a wide collar, three buttons on the back, and piping, which circled under her breast. It hung to her perfectly curved calves. She would never wear the floor-length veil made of checkered gauze trimmed with sparkles.

The familiar dress was all Kent saw of Ellie from a distance the next day as she stepped onto the train at dawn departing for Chicago. Ellie never looked back. He had begged the few stars above to bring her back. When he heard the train's whistle blow one long, last time, she was gone.

***

Today on an unusually hot summer day, she moved closer to Kent and reached for his big hands with long skinny fingers. He shook his head, still in disbelief that Ellie had walked away.

She had been his sweetheart since first grade, sharing a table on the front row of the classroom as teacher's pet. As kids they had played hide-and-go-seek in the high stalks of endless wheat fields, and they traded their first kisses under the tender age of ten in the pecan grove. In the high school band, they marched flirting as they played French horns. Seen as darlings in the eyes of the town's grown folks, they were a couple destined for a happy life together. The same people later sneered and prodded Kent for an explanation for why Ellie had left. Kent waited for her return week by week and year by year.

She withdrew her outreached hands, and he smiled at her feeling the uncomfortable tension building inside the pit of his stomach. She had his attention and looked into his dark brown eyes surrounded by clear whites. His smile to Ellie was like a hundred passionate kisses and she felt butterflies. Yet she was another man's wife, and in Kent's eyes they could be only friends, but nothing more.

Ellie was buying time with her silence, hoping for his forgiveness. These fleeting moments together were enough to sustain her wish for the right chance to correct her wrongs. One day soon, she would tell him her mistakes.

She was happy he could make their weekly meeting, always on Sundays, at four o'clock after dinner. It was

Ellie's routine to purposefully cook a big meal each Sunday, so she could tell her husband, Manny Clayton, she needed to walk it off. Ellie had skirted out of the house, leaving Manny to his Sunday paper on the porch. She walked the road northward until she disappeared across a field that bordered a fence row full of wild sunflowers. Over a pasture, she went on another road hidden by trees and made a jagged route through a rolling field. She sometimes varied her path around an old house where no one lived until she reached the thicket of tall pine trees. The thicket was full of broken stumps, briers, and low branches. There she stayed on the trail that she had used as a child to make her way to the barn, resting undisturbed in a no-man's land of tall brush.

Since returning, Ellie had visited the abandoned barn each Sunday afternoon, as they had as lovers long ago, hoping Kent would show. She had been four months back in Chester when bad news about Kent's younger brother James provided an opening. On this dark day in Kent's life, Ellie remembered as kids that they would settle their hurts in the privacy of the barn. She calculated his refuge would be the barn, and surprised him by appearing there. He took her into his arms while the heartbreaking telegram was still in his hands. Ellie comforted him. Kent needed to share his burden, and the Sunday meetings began. After that, stealing away to their favorite sneak-away as children was their secret.

✳✳✳

Today, she looked frantic. He could tell by the crinkle in her forehead that something was wrong.

"I'm afraid I can't have children. I'll never be a mother," she said when he saw her looking at him.

Kent stayed silent, unsure how to respond.

"I've been married now for over two years and nothing. I don't think it'll ever happen," she said with her teeth tight, exasperated.

After two years of trying to start a family and since returning to Chester, a place she hated, Ellie wondered if she was being punished for leaving Kent. And for what she did to their baby. She began to cry large tears from the corner of her eyes, and cupped her hands to her face.

"It's so hard being here. I need a child to go on." Ellie sniffled as the burden of her past choked her. She was hot and thirsty from the brisk walk.

Kent felt for her, but continued to lean on the post giving it all his weight. He crossed his arms and consolingly said, "It's going to be OK, Ellie."

"You don't understand," she said tearfully in fear of the past. "I've..., I've," she started as her sixth sense rose to attention. "I might not be able to because..." Her voice trailed off suddenly as the thought of Kent not forgiving her took over.

Knowing that he did not know about the baby made her return to Chester a bit bearable. If Ellie told him the truth, she worried that it would be Kent walking out of her life this time.

"I had no idea I would end up here again. Forgive me." Ellie switched gears and whispered.

"It's OK," Kent countered. Then he added, "Would you adopt, if you have to?"

His words stung.

***

Before returning to Chester, Ellie lived a perfect life in Chicago miles away from the troubles of Chester. She had peace. Now, her world was crashing down in the tiny town as she grew further away from her husband, fearing the secrets of the past.

Ellie's life took a hundred and eighty-degree aboutface and began to unravel when a call, in the same area code as Chester, blinked on the telephone caller ID. She and Manny had just returned from a fabulous Broadway show at the Schubert Theatre. Laughing as they swung into the condo, Ellie's red painted fingernail reached for the recorder's play button. She stopped midway as she recognized that the whole hidden story of her life in Chester probably waited at her fingertips.

"Let's have coffee and ice cream," Ellie said, rushing past the answering machine. She grabbed Manny's hand to detour him into the kitchen.

"Someone called?" He paused and hit the play button, pulling Ellie to his side for a hug.

She held her breath as he wrapped his arms around her knowing it was someone reeling off the facts of her past life in Chester. Beads of sweat formed around her mouth, with the reality that in a flash her life could change. She could not remember ever having calls from this area code before. Surely, what she had run away from over twenty years ago was closing in on her now.

The man's voice from the answering machine was mature and strong. "Hello, this call is for Manny Clayton, I'm an attorney."

Life-threatening thoughts flooded her mind, and she left Manny's arms. Ellie wanted to leave the room, but she was paralyzed with fear. She prayed that the caller had no facts of her last days in Chester, and her confused sense put her in a momentary trance.

The voice continued, "Sir, I have bad news. I'm very sorry you have to find out this way, but I'm following the law."

The word "law" cut Ellie like a knife. She felt the shortness of breath as she sat down afraid the truth was about to come out. Manny was curious, although he looked more worried. They both wondered who it could be. Manny stood still as a statue, hanging on each word.

"Please, call me as soon as you get this message if it's before 7:30 p.m. tonight. Otherwise reach me first thing tomorrow at..."

Ellie panicked not listening as the numbers trailed to silence. The machine went numb and then clicked off.

"Are you OK?" she managed to utter as her shaky hand hit unconsciously the remote control. The late night news theme pierced the silence.

"It leaves me wondering... Gosh, what a way to end the evening," Manny mumbled as the caller's words continued to play in his mind.

"No ice cream, let's just go to bed." Ellie hugged him scared to death of the ghost in her closet and the reason for the call. What would she do? What could she do?

It was already too late to call, but her torture would be slow and long until morning. Ellie turned the TV off and left Manny replaying the call. He listened several times to the man's delivery for clues and finally wrote the number on a yellow sticky pad.

Upstairs while dressing for bed, Ellie toyed with the idea of canceling her morning consulting session at work and staying home to hear what the Southern caller had to say. She wondered, "Who would do this after so many years?" Ellie slipped under the covers as her mind went fast through the past.

The next morning, she woke up tired. Her night had been restless. The covers were tangled around her legs when the alarm clock came on like a freight train. Manny was already in the bathroom. She could hear him brushing his teeth. In the little time left before he would return the call, Ellie prayed that what had haunted her for over twenty years would not take her back to Chester. Her mind raced for a solution and a response to Manny as she faced the inevitable news reaching him.

With red eyes, Manny scuffled out of the bathroom in his house shoes, still in his robe. He had tossed and turned half as much as Ellie.

"Babe, I'm going to make the call. I want you with me, Sweetie," he said, reaching for the receiver near her pillow. Ellie sat up wiping sleep from her eyes.

"Sure, I'm right here," she uttered, wondering for how long she would be, if the caller told everything.

17

Manny dialed the numbers written on the yellow sticky. With the phone to his mouth, he looked uncomfortable as he asked for the attorney.

Manny listened closely to the man on the other end of the line. "Mr. Clayton, I've been hired to handle your grandfather's affairs. He died one week ago. I'm sorry to be the one to tell you."

"Oh, my goodness, he died a whole week ago," Manny said, plopping to the bed and pushing Ellie back as he scooted for space.

"Yes and he has already been buried." Coughing from chain smoking, he stated, "It was your grandfather's request that no one notify any of his children or have a funeral."

"Oh, Uh," Manny stuttered, trying to process what he had heard.

"As heartless as it may sound, I must tell you he insisted on his grave being undisclosed and unmarked," the man cut in.

Ellie surmised it was not what she had worried about all night, but serious. Someone had died. Manny continued listening and Ellie waited, patting and rubbing her hand down his back.

The attorney's details told of Manny's grandfather checking himself into the local nursing home after covering his furniture, turning off the utilities, and ordering that the plans of the new house be completed. He had put his business in order years ago willing all he owned to Manny. Although he later wanted to add, once he was senile and mumbling, that the new house go to a lady name Claudine. The attorney steadfastly refused to make the change, but out of concern, he had canvassed the whole town for anyone named Claudine, finding no one.

"One last thing, do you know anyone named Claudine?" He picked Manny's brain to no avail. Manny was half listening now, thinking of how to break the news to his mother.

It had been a part of the will that the attorney make this call two weeks after the old man's death, but he felt sorry for the surviving relatives and called a week early. Manny's grandfather had intentionally died alone. And worse yet, he was buried in an undisclosed place out of spite, so that his clan of eight children would recall his warning to never come back when they left the farm going North.

Manny sorrowed for his own mother whose father had passed still resenting his children. As a young boy, he had heard the tales of them being disowned for their running away, but the reality of his grandfather actually carrying out his ugly threats this way hurt.

Manny's aunts and uncles often quoted their father who had said that to desert the land of their forefathers was cowardly. At family reunions which he continuously failed to attend, they repeated his story of how their family went from being slaves, then sharecroppers, and paying tenfold for what any land was worth. He would say they had walked away from their heritage for what he called pie-in-the-sky modern day comforts, failing to stick with the land. He shouted at them to never come back.

Manny's mother sometimes cried from her memories of him being adamant that she stayed away, once she chose to live in Chicago. His mother was so heartbroken that she sent Manny to visit him when he would allow her. That was her only connection to her goading father.

After Manny hung up, he leaned into Ellie telling her the gist of the conversation. She soothed him, brushing her hand over his hair.

"I'm so sorry," Ellie whispered.

Quite bewildered, Manny called his retired parents and stoically said, "I'm coming over, please get the family together and tell them that it's very important. I'll be there in twenty minutes." His mother knew it was grave news, hearing the tone in her son's voice.

Ellie bolted to the bathroom relieved and quickly jumped into the shower. Water ran down her body taking her senseless thoughts down the drain.

Two months later, an envelope from Albany, Georgia came in the mail. Unbeknownst to Ellie, what rested between the long distance bill and the latest edition of Essence would reveal the secrets of her past.

It was like a nightmare when Ellie learned from her husband that his grandfather had generously willed him a 300-acre farm in Chester, Georgia—her hometown. Manny stunned her as he read the legal papers—County of Maze and City of Chester. Before Ellie could say that she once lived in Chester, Manny continued reading the pages aloud.

He excitedly flashed the pages quickly one behind the other paraphrasing out loud to her, "In order to receive the inheritance, I have to farm the land for four years. '...Said land located in Chester at Route 2, County of Maze.'"

"For four years," he repeated, emphasizing the number four, looking at Ellie. "Darn shrewd!"

Ellie's mouth was open and her eyes wide.

"Well, me a farmer," he said, half surprised at the strict terms and stipulations, thinking that his one-eyed grandfather was very cunning.

His last testament was meant to keep the land in the family even if it was necessary to snatch one of his fancy kinfolk from the North.

On the fast track at IBM, Manny was a tall dark and lean computer analyst, driven by his career. Facing a choice to farm in Chester was like hitting a foul ball in his shot to the top. This curve in their plans coming from the grave of his grandfather would change their lives. Manny had only seen him twice in his life during long summer visits to Chester. The first time he was a seven-year-old boy. The second and last visit Manny made as a teenager, after his grandfather had lost an eye.

Manny was the favorite of the short, dark-skinned, wide-chested man who spoke to people like he was a five-star general in the army. He was rewarded heavily for taking the time to visit him below the gnat line even though he did it primarily for adventure. Manny had been the only grandchild to do so after eight out of eight of his mother's siblings trickled North after the war, leaving the land and its way of life. Knowing that accepting the conditions could derail his career, he still felt pulled by the honor.

He remembered the barefoot summers spent in Chester, surreal with freedom and frolic. Eating half-ripe peaches and whole watermelons were a daily routine. He could holler as loud as he wanted, and no one would hear. Sounds that echoed endlessly and bounced off the trees thrilled him. Picking sunflowers to play she-loves-me-she-loves-me-not was Manny's favorite pastime on his summer visits.

He had enjoyed the farm as a youngster, but moving there was something to think about. Changing lifestyles and leaving Chicago reminded him of the old comedy sitcom "Green Acres." But nothing about moving to Chester was funny, it was decision time.

Still skimming through the document, Manny was mesmerized with the huge inheritance. There were 300 acres of farmland, two houses, lots of heavy farming equipment and even a nearly new automobile. Plus, the will proposed paying him a sizable salary for two years.

"Wow!" he yelled while holding a copy of what could change their future.

Manny felt fortunate, but also guilty. "Why me?" he thought, when his mother and all seven of her siblings were still alive. Because everyone had deserted his grandfather to live in Chicago, he pulled the weakest link he knew of, Manny. The cantankerous old man never forgave his children and departed this world having gotten even.

For the moment and now until he decided, the land, the houses, and money were his and Ellie's in black and white. It was all theirs for the taking but under major conditions.

Manny hastily called the local attorney who was probating the will to estimate the value of his inheritance.

He was astounded that the land alone was worth at least a half a million dollars.

He placed the phone temporarily on his thigh and mouthed to Ellie, "A half million."

Ellie turned her back seeing the skyline and traced the tall buildings to steady her nerves. Manny was way too excited about the will to notice Ellie's fears.

He winked once at his wife as he hung up the telephone and said, "Well, we have to decide one way or the other and soon. I can't believe he used an iron fist from the hereafter."

He chuckled and set the documents in the center of living room's glass table, intending to read the attached hand written notes later. Manny was still oblivious to Ellie's concern.

After two weeks of trying to make a decision, Manny debated about taking a leave of absence for one year to see if he could handle farming. The terms were to farm the land he rationalized. The will was absent a definition for successful farming. So Manny thought he could hang out in the fresh country air on a sunny porch reading, if he wanted to for four years, sell the land after appreciation, and come out far ahead of his income at IBM for the same period of time.

The windfall urged a "yes." They had to go. Financially it made good sense. Manny would accept the duty of his generation by showing the strongest gesture of respect, which was to try and keep what could now rightfully be called the Clayton land in the family. Yet no matter how much farming had meant to his grandfather, after adhering to the four-year term, they would move back to Chicago.

He mulled over the terms for another two weeks. Then one morning while Ellie was reading on the plush soft sofa, he returned after taking a long jog on the lakefront and announced, "We must leave Chicago by early spring for the planting season."

He was proud of recalling when to plant from his grandfather's notes on farming, which had strained his eyes while he read the odd long skinny handwriting. Manny slung his sweaty T-shirt into the powder room and kicked off his running shoes without taking his eyes off Ellie.

Ellie dropped her magazine and stood up, swallowing hard. "Go back!" She screamed.

It was as if a ghost had sneaked up behind her and pulled her face to face with what she had run away from long ago.

"Go back, to Chester!" She gazed past her husband with her lips pressed angrily.

A chill went down her back. The fear burning her eyes turned the beige walls of their fancy condo dark brown. An upper middle class existence in Chicago suited her dreams of a lifetime. Their return to Chester was not a matter of money to her, but the freedom to be Ellie.

"Ellie, it makes sense, it really does," Manny said, trying to convince her to see his side. "Honey, look at me," Manny remarked wanting her attention.

She jerked around to face him.

With their stares locked, he interjected, "Sweetheart don't you have people there?"

"No!" Ellie cut him off, "All my family moved away. I came here for a reason."

She needed to sit down. He caught her arm and guided her to the black leather sofa and against his bare chest. From the highrise's living room window the skyview of Southside Chicago was behind them as they hugged. Hiding from memories of the past, she buried her face in his chest.

"Tell me about your days in Chester," Manny offered softly, breaking the silence.

Ellie spoke as she raised her head to look into his eyes. "I didn't like it there. Moving back will not be good for me." She gazed long at Manny without blinking and continued. "My mother left me there with her wretched old common law husband on a farm. I was only sixteen years old, still in high school. He was mean and always unhappy. If it hadn't been for the nice neighbors, I would've been alone. After one year of living in that spiteful man's house, I left and tried to find my mother here in Chicago. I never did. She just left me there like a lost sheep." Soft tears rolled slowly down her heavily made-up cheeks. Ellie shuddered at the night of screaming when her mother left her.

She took a long deep breath and feigned a headache by touching her temples. To hide her tears she looked down at the end of her black Lycra leggings to her tiny orange-red toes in need of a new topcoat of polish. She hoped Manny would be quiet. His hot breath moved purposefully through her long hair and to her pretend headache spot. Feeling him kiss her, Ellie knew Chester was days away, and she cried aloud. For now, she wanted no more questions, so she eased from his side, snatched up her magazine and went to bed early. She wept.

Ellie was edgy for three days, still refusing to go back to Chester. Until then they had been comfortable with what they knew about each other. But the day would come when Manny would learn things he never knew about her. Ellie had intentionally left the past behind.

Manny had lived in Chicago all his life. From a family of go-getters, he had made straight A's in high school, earning a full scholarship to Northwestern. Contemporary jazz was his favorite music. He was a non-smoker who enjoyed fine wines, rarely taking a drink of hard liquor. Manny treated her special—like a lady, and Ellie fell madly in love with him. She married Manny without a second thought. Ellie was anxiously trying to get pregnant and have his first child, when the news of returning to Chester came crashing down.

Manny knew Ellie was originally from a small town in Georgia, but she never gave it a name, simply speaking of it as a small town. She had lived in Chicago since she was a teenager with her cousin Mae. He met Ellie seven years ago and they dated for five, then married. He liked her tasty Southern-style cooking, especially collard greens and homemade cornbread called hocakes. She was beautiful, sensual and made him feel special. She was the one to settle down with. Manny knew without a doubt that he had found the woman of his dreams.

In the bedroom, Ellie pushed her face under a pillow trying to stifle a wail. Hearing the name of the small town she had tried to forget sent waves through her stomach, a message from her first love, Kent. Ellie feared she had smothered her emotions for him. Life with Manny was good, but was it good enough to erase the forbidden memories, which flooded her mind after learning of his roots in Chester?

Since the will, Ellie had not witnessed a day without thinking of her life in Chester, Kent, and the child she was carrying when she left for Chicago. Six months later, Manny traded his button-down suit for overalls and a tractor. Ellie was in the same place she started from and desperate to keep her secrets.

✳✳✳

Now in the barn, shadows were building from a missing piece of the tin roof above their heads, forming a jagged chasm between them. When she crossed it, she stood face to face with Kent wanting to apologize for leaving, but instead she omitted the whole truth. Shame shook her inside and paralyzed her with guilt. Moving back here was sheer punishment as it was a daily reminder of the baby and the vow she made before God. Her vow of marriage to another man was like a line drawn in the sand and something sacred, which Kent was not willing to cross.

She wrongfully hungered for his touch, thinking it would win his forgiveness. When she did, Kent would not feed her hunger and honored her choice to marry someone else. She had made decisions that they all must live with forever.

Ellie moved slowly toward him. He heard the hay crushing under her feet like she was gliding through Fall leaves. She searched his eyes wanting him to care so much that he would forgive her past mistakes. But she was unwilling to ask him until she felt sure he would forgive her.

"If you only knew what it was like for me to be back here. I wish....I desperately want to have a child," Ellie said, judging whether now was the right time.

"I'm really sorry that you haven't gotten pregnant. You'd be a good mother."

"I've got to soon," Ellie sighed.

He cleared his throat.

"There's a time for everything. Don't worry, it'll happen," Kent said.

Not caring to respond, Ellie was tiring of the tornado of emotions about the past. To have peace he had to come around soon. Standing a foot apart, she lifted her arms to embrace him. Ellie began to lean closer when they heard a voice echoing in the distance beyond the trees.

"Ellie! Ellie!"

It was Manny who brought Ellie back to Chester in the shadows of what she faced, making her live as the very words she had spoken she would never be—a farmer's wife. Hearing him call, she froze. There was much more dirt than his land from George Custer Banks, the man who people in town had referred to as "Killer Banks." As children they had used an ugly name for him. Almost everyone had because of the way his pop eyes bulged when he was angry, which was most of the time.

Manny's land sat adjacent to the 400-acres of Kent's family. The old barn sheltering Ellie and Kent was on the northside divider line between their two farms. The Vinsons had farmed for three generations as well as Manny's folk. For Kent's dad, Sonny, owning the land was like a knighting of southern success. It was Sonny's land by birthright and a haunting promise he made to his father.

Sonny, an aging farmer, had a head full of pepper gray hair and deep-set eyes. As a widower, he watched the news three times a day and played bingo by himself. Sonny was delighted that Kent had followed in his footsteps. The Vinson men were proud farmers, attending meetings and fraternizing with the other landowners.

The group had dwindled to half of the numbers from a decade ago. Having a new black farmer was unheard of, so Manny shined as a newcomer with his business background, but he was quiet. A class action was in progress, and Manny quickly learned a lot about the abuses farmers were likely to suffer. Hearing the others talk about the injustices done, he tried hard to measure up to his grandfather's farming. Manny had fast awakened to the reality that farmers could not plant whatever they wanted or how much they wanted. There was a system, which allotted corn, peanuts, soybean, cotton, tobacco and even sunflower fields by acreage, everything.

After hearing more and more about the case, Manny began to consider joining the suit on his grandfather's behalf. But before deciding to join the class action, he knew he needed to gather witnesses and check his facts with Sonny who was a strong pillar of honesty in the community.

Sonny, like Manny's grandfather, had stood the test of time as farmers. Sonny always insisted on fairness doing business by the book. When he faced unfair prices or did not get the treatment he thought was due, Sonny held out and had a Plan B. Killer Banks had been a heavy-handed dealer, but he was nonetheless quite successful.

Sonny succeeded by playing squarely on the dime, never wavering from the right side of right or being an honorable man. But times had changed as Sonny prepared to turnover the land to Kent and his youngest son, James, by inheritance. These days, it took more to do less, even for Sonny as wise a leader as he was in the rural farming community, giving a willing hand to others. The spotlight was on him upon the Claytons' arrival in Chester. Manny's grandfather had given specific instructions to him to seek out Sonny for help.

The three men had gathered on a Saturday evening after a class action session, minus Ellie when Manny met the Vinsons. She had avoided going along with Manny to meet their neighbors. Unsure of what returning would hold for her, she needed privacy to see Kent alone. Ellie's feelings were mixed with years of pain and hiding her past. But even in the secrecy of the barn, she still could not lift the veil of her deceit and tell the truth.

***

The sound of Manny's voice was still ringing in their ears. Their time together had escaped.

"It's time to go," Kent stated as he moved toward the opened space that was once a huge door for herding horses or occasionally a borrowed cotton picker.

Leaving the barn to head home, Ellie reached for Kent grazing his plaid shirt near his biceps. The touch offered without words was an understanding that they would meet again next Sunday after supper as they had for months. The unspoken bond continued and this weekly system of communication worked flawlessly in their secret place of the past. No one else knew.

Kent said his good-byes to Ellie and headed North back to his farm. He looked around above his head and saw the moon and sun in opposite skies. As he walked away, both seemed to escort him. A short distance further, Kent turned and waved one more time at Ellie and then at the moon and sun, wondering if they too were lovers that would always be apart. Was it their destiny?

CHAPTER TWO

*O*n a clear mid-July Tuesday, Sonny reached into his leaning mailbox where a little figure with a fishing pole sat on top and brought out a single letter. It was from his son, James Phillip Vinson. Today was the first time he ever received a letter from his thirty-one-year-old son. Heat hit the back of his neck and began to burn.

The letter was postmarked June 6, 1997. It was addressed to him in uneven felt tip scribbles, but he knew it was his son's hand before he saw "James." In the middle of the pasty envelope, the complete rural route address numbers were missing. Under Sonny's name was a line with only the city, Chester and the state, Georgia. No zip code. Expecting bad news, he held it up toward the sun and shook it for any clue. Sonny saw one word through the thin envelope, and he knew something was wrong. Fear shot through his bones and rushed him to numbness. Sonny stopped dead in his tracks.

The house was a few yards away in a curve off the road leading to a huge pecan grove at the end. The summer heat had withered the grass, making brown spots in the yard. Flowers planted by his late wife, Stella, bowed their heads and thirsted for rain as his boots grew heavy taking tiny steps. A hummingbird flew over Sonny's head racing in a hurry for a leafy Chinaberry tree while he moved slowly, stepping on a few small round berries. Dreading the moment he would open the letter, his heart pounded like a drum.

"Kent!" he shouted to his oldest son. He had left him sitting in his LaZy Boy chair watching the six o'clock local news. He yelled louder a second time without listening for an answer, "Kent!" The words echoed back-to-back like rap music bouncing off the distant trees.

Alarmed, Kent jumped up juggling his warm supper plate of reheated macaroni and cheese with cubed steak on his lap. He balanced it with burning fingertips safely down and quickly followed the intense voice outside. He saw his stalwart dad standing limp as cooked noodles with his head wobbling and eyes glazed. Sonny was buckling to the ground.

Kent raised dust running to him and put his arms around Sonny's shoulders.

"Oh my! Oh my, Dad!" Kent was looking for rolled back eyes and any sign of discoloration. "What's wrong with you? Is it your heart? Please be OK." Sonny staggered in his son's arms as Kent quickly straddled him.

Sonny garbled his words and dropped the letter. Kent's eyes followed the object as it settled to the ground. It landed between his feet planted on both sides of Sonny.

"Dad, tell me something," Kent said, acknowledging the envelope with a glance.

He could see James's handwriting in thick uneven black marks written like a child practicing the alphabets. His brother's single name was alone in the left-hand corner and absent any return address on the envelope.

Sonny stared aimlessly into nowhere leaning on Kent.

"Let's get you inside." Kent aided his father toward the house, leaving the letter for the moment. "That's it. Keep moving. Slowly, you're doing fine," he coached, carefully guiding Sonny the short distance to the front door. He moved them along stopping to plant Sonny's lifeless body again and again until they reached the doorsteps.

Kent pushed the screen door open and held it with his right hip before they dragged like tired soldiers into the den. The room was full of men's stuff. Old tattered and dirt-clumped field boots lined the doorway. A wooden coat rack held two long sleeve striped shirts worn to fend off mosquitoes. In front of a TV with wide rabbit antenna ears, a thick corduroy green LaZy Boy was perched. On a lamp table were Sonny's snuff and spit cup with mostly dried ink pens next to a scratch pad. Matches, scattered on the mantel like wasted toothpicks, had long been used to light the fireplace still full of last winter's ashes.

Kent gingerly placed his father onto the sofa. Sonny reached for the armrest and missed it five times. Clearing his throat to maintain his bearings, Kent put his hand on top of Sonny's and held it there.

When Sonny seemed comfortable, Kent said, "I'll be right back, don't move."

Kent left the room on the run and drew a glass of water from the kitchen sink. Running back, he stumbled over a round corded rug in front of the kitchen entrance, spilling water.

"Here, Dad drink some." Kent held the glass for him.

Sonny took a sip. He leaned his head back and focused on the ceiling fan spinning. Sonny remembered the day a defiant James left for San Francisco, a young seaman in the navy. Sonny had showered James with unwanted World War II stories about him and his old bunk buddies, loudly calling their last names and titles, basically talking to the wind. He occasionally saluted while conjuring up the memories. Hearing the name Casselberry was a sure signal to escape before Sonny began reliving the war like it was yesterday.

Turning eighteen, James earned the right to leave the farm. Without feeling guilty on that day, he took the privilege of tuning out the old war stories he had heard time after time.

James, a narrow small-framed guy, hated farm work. He was practically helpless doing his chores. Although a bit brainy and book crazy, he rebelled against Sonny and wore long hair and a pierced ear. James disliked dirty hands and had cologne on when he feed the hogs. He dreaded the hot, sweaty sun-up-to-sundown summer workdays. His attitude made it sure as death and taxes to Sonny that he would never be a farmer. James left without a second thought as soon as he legally could.

Sonny had tussled to control James by insisting that he stay and farm the land. Once Sonny promised his father to hold tight to their land, he never compromised. That included James' request to join the navy. Sonny was determined to keep the farmland in the Vinson family, and he came down hard against James leaving.

Their land was one thing Sonny counted on. He trusted that it would be for his future generations. It once saved his life and then gave him the assurance he had bit into the pie of the American Dream. Seeing many others struggle to win over and over again their land purchased with hard labor, he dared not to waiver on his promise.

James, his youngest son, would one day inherit most of the acreage. It was a Vinson tradition to give the baby in the family the greatest land portion. Now waiting for the strange letter, Sonny wondered if James would ever come back to the farm.

Usually, Sonny heard from his youngest son every other week. But thinking back, he realized that lately, James' calls had been much more sporadic since the beginning of the summer.

"Darn it," Sonny blamed the summer harvesting for keeping him too busy to see the obvious.

His son had needed him even though in his recent telephone calls home, James had said he was doing fine, not once indicating that anything was wrong.

Realizing that he had missed a cue, Sonny recalled James was actively planning his fifteen-year high school class reunion, which was held two months ago. Yet he missed it. Why would James be a no-show when he worked so hard with the reunion committee for a whole year gathering addresses and soliciting his lost classmates? Questioning the cancelled visit, Sonny knew that it did not add up. He had provided him assistance by locating several of the hard-to-find classmates, tracking down their parents' or great aunts' telephone numbers. It was easy to get him the contacts, since everyone knew everyone or was somehow kinfolk however remote the lineage.

When James confirmed his plans to arrive home for the reunion week, they had looked for him. But he never came. On what would have been the first night of the reunion, James called with a vague explanation that something had come up, and he just could not make it. Second-guessing the course of events with the letter arriving, Sonny realized that James had been too excited about the class reunion to simply dismiss it. He was senior class vice president. Stressing, Sonny felt the letter could not be good news by any means as he rubbed his left hand nervously along the arm of the sofa.

"Dad, I'm right here," Kent spoke softly, kneeling at his father's feet. "Can I get you anything else?"

"No, son," Sonny remarked barely projecting an audible sound.

To make his father comfortable he took off Sonny's combat boots, unwinding the strings that circled his ankles to keep out field dirt. He rolled his socks into tight balls and stuck one inside each boot.

"You're not feeling any pain, are you?" Kent inquired, deciding to check his dad's pulse.

Sonny grunted.

Kent pulled out his pocket watch and placed three fingers on Sonny's inside wrist. Watching the second hand ticking, he counted. When he was finished, Kent held onto his father's hand as if Sonny were a little boy.

"You want me to get the letter and read it? Dad?" Kent asked, standing up and waiting for Sonny's response. His knees popped as he stood, becoming aware that the TV was going. He snapped it off to hear.

Sonny was silent.

Knowing that Sonny felt the letter was bad news, Kent pushed the screen door open and headed down the footpath to the mailbox. He traced his steps to where his eyes fell on the white envelope. He took a deep breath looking at it before bending. The earth seemed still as he smelled the gigantic gardenia bushes his mother had planted near the mailbox.

Picking up the letter, he noticed that practically a month had passed since James penned the letter. It was just plain odd. The post office miraculously did its job. He thought they were lucky to get his mail without a zip code or a complete address. The small rural town was on somebody's map.

Kent placed his forefinger underneath the seal and ripped a jagged opening with one quick jerk. He slowly took out and unfolded the eight and a half by eleven sheet of lined paper. He read:

EXPECT SUNSHINE

Dad,

I'm dying. I was afraid of what you would think, so I stayed away. There is much grief in this world. I have AIDS. I have arranged for my caretaker Debbie to take care of my affairs in San Francisco. You may contact her at the Mercy Hospice for my body. Don't try to come. It is too late. Nothing and no one can help me.

Love,

James

Kent crushed the paper in a tight fist. He glanced toward the gardenia bushes and thought of his dead mother, and how devastated she would have been to hear this. The life of her baby was threatened. Looking away from the unbelievable news typed off center in weak strokes, Kent viewed his world of the white wood frame house, the massive oak trees in the yard, and their land as far as the eye could see. He had been happy in his peaceful world of farming until Ellie returned four months ago and now this.

Unwilling to trust the words on a simple piece of paper torn from a tablet, he half smoothed the crumpled letter and read it a second time. Picturing his younger brother, Kent tapped his chin in disbelief. He saw that the grass needed mowing and the hedges trimming. He pumped his chest with four short deep breaths of air to control his emotions. Kent wanted to burst into a mad scream, but he focused on building a reserve of strength for his father.

Moving slowly to the house, Kent fought back tears, closing his eyes. He realized the actual news could kill his seventy-eight-year-old dad. The letter was like what Sonny suspected. But he could not he tell the man resting in the house that his youngest son was dying.

Kent looked at the paper he had balled up, refusing to give in to the reality that James would soon die. The news was too much for him. What would it do to Sonny?

Flustered that time had been squandered by the incomplete address, Kent panicked wondering if James was already dead. They both had to be with him, soon.

Kent hurried into the house with the screen door flapping behind him making a loud noise. Sonny's eyes followed him as he came to the sofa. He saw his oldest son's face flushed—the tattletale sign to expect the worst.

"Dad, it isn't good news." Kent shook his head, holding the letter. "We've gotta leave right away."

He could tell Sonny did not want the details. He was just satisfied that his son was alive. Ready to rush to San Francisco, Sonny's head moved up and down, bobbing like a fishhook as he caught onto the tiniest bit of hope that he would help James.

"He'll be alright once I get there," Sonny said, jumping up barefoot and pointing his finger to the ceiling. The old man's full body shuddered while looking at the letter in Kent's hand.

The fact of the pasty white envelope was sinking in that the next moment could be the very last for James. They had to leave for San Francisco immediately. Kent called the nearest airport, which provided them the fastest connection to the West Coast. After desperately trying every airline, he found that it was too late for them to fly today.

With the telephone to his ear, Kent crouched on a stool with a yellow writing tablet on his knees taking the flight information. His pen ran out of ink, peppering the already tender situation with frustration. He threw it across the room and took a second one from the lamp table. Their departure plans were to drive three hours in the morning to Atlanta and take the first available direct flight to San Francisco. Sonny hovered close to him as Kent held the telephone, writing.

"Get the first flight available. Don't care what it costs." Sonny declared, seeing Kent's written flight numbers and times. After barreling his request, Sonny began to pace.

Kent held the telephone between his ear and shoulder, finalizing their departure time. He repeated, "1:00 p.m. is the earliest after 8:00 a.m. It works. Thanks."

"The earliest flight possible, Son." Sonny decoded the one-sided conversation as he stood near Kent's available ear.

Kent stopped talking to the voice on the other end with the receiver still pressed to his ear. The father and son looked at each other. He nodded for Sonny's agreement. When Sonny stared back without a word, Kent hunched his shoulder signaling he had done his best and hung up the telephone.

The room was quiet except the steady humming of the cuckoo clock that ceased coo cooing last peanut season. Sonny sat down on the sofa next to Kent's miniature stool and took the letter from him. Placing it on his lap, he smoothed the crinkled paper some more. The words stunned Sonny. He stayed on the sofa reading the letter over and over until after midnight, when Kent guided him to bed, insisting they sleep for tomorrow's journey.

Walking in a straight line to his room, Sonny carried the letter in his twisted, heavily knuckled hands. The broad-shouldered man of the best crop in town was wrestling with a killer disease he had heard about on TV. He could not sleep. A desktop lamp stuck in the crevice of his headboard shone on the letter that he read continuously while sitting fully dressed in bed behind his closed door. He had pulled the bedcovers onto the floor earlier saying his prayers. Too weak to replace the lightweight bedspread, Sonny crawled into his private space, which had provided comfort and peace until now. Restless and weary, he begged for sleep while staring at the letter and listening to Kent pace the floor.

The next morning, Sonny dressed before the sun rose. He put on black trousers, a white shirt, a brown belt and Hush Puppy shoes. He was ready for the three-hour winding ride to Atlanta. When daylight pushed through the curtains Sonny had left opened, it provide him with an urge to expect sunshine on the day he would see his sick and dying child.

He leaned on the edge of the bed near his side table. Trying hard to erase the fact that the letter was real, he stared at family pictures on his nightstand, which sat on a plastic runner in dusty frames. His favorites were one of his late wife, Stella, with her legs crossed wearing thick rolled bobby socks, holding a purse under her arm. Another was of him and the boys at age ten and two standing in front of his tractor.

If the letter had not come, it would have been his day to make routine buys at the hardware store, nails, light bulbs and a screwdriver. Worrying about the fate of his child, he tapped his Hush Puppies on the wooden floor, seeing they needed shining, shaking his head and wanting to trade places with his youngest son. Light crept under his bedroom door from the hallway where he heard Kent slamming drawers while packing. Sonny resisted moving as he waited anxiously for Kent to knock.

Sonny was the kind of person who, once dressed, was ready to go. Many times he and Kent went to church in separate vehicles because Sonny was dressed first and too ready to wait.

It was barely light outside when Kent peeked at his father. As soon as the door creaked, Sonny was on his feet with keys and hat in hand.

"It's too early," Kent said, reaching for Sonny's packed bag, hoping to calm him.

Sonny ignored him and left the bedroom on Kent's heels following him into the main living area adjacent to the kitchen. Seeing his dad so feisty, Kent went to the kitchen without stopping and began searching cabinets for Sonny's high blood pressure medicine, which Sonny took irregularly.

"Here, Dad take this," he offered.

"I should take it with food," Sonny said, holding out his hand for the pill.

"We can eat," Kent urged.

"No, no let's go!" Sonny said, nearly tripping as he grabbed his bag. The old man bent from years of farm work shot straight to the front door.

"How about breakfast in town as usual? We've got time." Kent signaled to Sonny with a nod and took the duffel bag from his dad's shoulder.

He turned out the lights and closed the door behind them without Sonny agreeing. Kent planned to eat breakfast in town. Although neither one wanted to cook nor eat, it was necessary for the stamina to make the trip. They were speechless during the ride in.

It was 7:00 a.m. when they entered Chester's only café. They were immediately seated in a booth by a window under bold colored curtains with large red hens and an egg basket design. A group of regulars lined the counter sipping strong coffee from brown ceramic mugs. Others were gathered around three small tables pressed against the back wall. The smell of bacon and onions permeated the place.

Kent ordered the house special for both of them: two eggs with sausage patties and a large bowl of grits. The order came promptly with their check. Sonny blessed their food and silently asked God to spare James until they could reach him later today. During breakfast, they sat across from each other numb on the squeaky seats.

In silence, Kent ate the last spoonful of his grits when he saw a different waitress coming toward them. She was a loud six-foot woman who ran the morning crew of waitresses. Everyone affectionately called her Tall Nancy. Most wanted to wring her neck for being nosey and the biggest town gossip.

"Good morning, y'aaawl," she said in a heavy southern drawl, disturbing the peace in the small café.

She reached their table planting her size tens hard on the speckled blue floor. Her scuffled shoe marks had streaked a path where she checked and bothered each table.

"How you?" Sonny spoke softly.

"Mister Wilkins is wondering what happened to yawl. It's Wednesday, right?" she asked puzzled, stretching her long neck side to side.

"We couldn't get to the hardware store today." Kent caught her eyes with a stealthy expression that meant leave them alone.

"I told him yawl would probably stop by here as usual, better go see what he wants." She urged them.

"We might if we have time." Kent smiled to ease any detection that something was wrong.

Sonny hung his head as Tall Nancy spoke, his eyes darting between the salt and pepper shakers. Tall Nancy continued smacking on chewing gum and looking around for her next victim. Kent reached his hand out to her with a five-dollar bill stacked on top of their check, hoping she would not need to come back. At arm's length she waited with a closed mouth annoyed with Chester's finest residents.

"Could you settle this for us? Thanks," Kent asked without looking into her face.

"What's the deal with you two?" Tall Nancy hollered at the top of her voice, pushing against Kent's arm.

The whole café focused on the window booth.

"Leave us be, Nancy." Kent began to get up.

Tall Nancy suspiciously put her rosy red lips to his ear and blabbered, "It's that darn telegram Mr. Wilkins got for yawl, ain't it?"

"If you knew something, why didn't you tell us?"

"Well, I was trying to stay out of yawl's business." Tall Nancy bit back. "It don't matter cause here he comes." She pointed at the wide body passing the window.

Mr. Wilkins stopped and peered in the café, cupping his hands around his eyes and pressed in on the glass. He saw Sonny sitting and tapped on the windowpane with two light thumps. Waving hello with fat fingers and shaking a yellow small envelope, Mr. Wilkins signaled that he was coming in to see them. He came in, turning partially sideways and his butt still scraped the doorframe.

Tall Nancy's loud voice carried through the place, "Here they go."

She pointed at them like they were strangers.

Kent met Mr. Wilkins halfway. "Morning, we were going to stop by before we left town," Kent said as he reached for the telegram.

Mr. Wilkins handed it to Kent with a pat on the back. "We get excited when one of these come our way. Here ya go. I hope it's good news," he said.

Kent thanked him and took it fearing the worst.

"It's marked urgent for the both of you." Aiming his short finger at the large stamped word, Mr. Wilkins said, "See, here."

He spun around speaking and waving at everybody. Mr. Wilkins walked away and bustled to the counter, obviously waiting for the news.

"Let's open it," Tall Nancy anxiously stuttered.

Kent backed her off with a stare. Then he sat back down in the booth next to his father and handed it to him without a word. Sonny took the telegram and opened it. On the paper in all bold and capital letters:

THE BODY OF JAMES PHILLIP VINSON
WILL ARRIVE WITHIN 48 HOURS TO
THE CARE OF SONNY AND/OR KENT VINSON
YOU MUST MAKE CLAIM UPON ARRIVAL.

Sonny slumped and cried out bumping his head on the window.

Tall Nancy shouted, "Lawd, have mercy!"

Everyone was alarmed. Leaving their places, they crowded around her and heard the news.

***

Back home, Kent marched his father to his iron post bed. Sonny had not said a word since he read the bad news. The overstuffed mattress sank under Sonny's weight as his feet lifted off the floor. Propping up his pillow, Kent assured him that he would handle James' body. A stunned and mourning father waved the son beside him away to be alone. Hoping his dad would be all right, Kent shut the bedroom door and waited for him to fall asleep. Two hours later he peered in Sonny's room. The old man was still.

Thinking that his father was asleep, Kent left to grieve. With the telegram in his hand he hurried out of the house, oblivious to his path, but straight to the abandoned barn. In the barn, he rested his tired, traveling bones on a bale of old hay, knowing he was all his father had now. He had lost his mother over thirty years ago. Memories of them came and went. He wept aloud, doubled over in sorrow. When he lifted his head, he saw Ellie and fell into her open arms. She was there consoling his hurt that James was gone forever.

The land had a history of running their loved ones away. As Kent melted into Ellie's breasts, he was sure the land was why she had left him and come back another man's wife. Since her return, Kent had thought about leaving his home and farming. The part of him that still loved her was desperate to leave. But how could he now in the shadows of James death?

As Ellie clutched her weeping old lover in her arms, it was a sad day, similar to when Sonny had lost his wife, Stella, giving birth to James. Sonny still blamed himself for Stella's death. He could not rest thinking about Stella, James and the promise.

***

It was June 1966. Stella was in her last month of pregnancy with James and whining to Sonny about having another child before leaving the farm to go North. Their talks about leaving the small town were heated, one-sided debates. She raged and he stalled. Stella loved Sonny, but everyone seemed to enjoy moving North, and she wanted to go desperately.

She despised Chester where giant grasshoppers walked the cotton rows in the drought season. And Gnats were everywhere like party confetti. She was tired dreaming of trips that were not taken. Pushing midlife and pregnant with James, Stella spoke up louder than ever, threatening to leave soon as the baby was born.

Sonny had sidestepped answering, holding on to the promise, which weighed on him like bricks. He begged for her understanding with watery eyes while reminding her of his promise to his father to stick with the farm.

"Break it!" Stella squawked pulling at her hair. Her mind was made up. She was leaving without him.

When Sonny was unable to change her mind about leaving him, he finally told Stella the whole story of what happened at Moccasin Pond that sealed his fate at age twenty-five. Hearing it, Stella understood and humbly accepted that Sonny's life was tied to the farm. She gave up all hope of leaving Chester.

Home alone on the day of delivery, Stella began to bleed as the baby's placenta pulled way. She bled heavily as she lay helpless for hours. When the sunset, Sonny should have been home. Stella had refused to scream out his name, seeing the weakening shadows slipped from the floor through the window holding hands with the setting sun, growing darker. Stella took the pain as Sonny continued to ride the fields.

Pitch dark, Sonny came in from plowing and found her on the floor. He hurried to his closet and pulled out the shotgun. He stumbled outside and fired twice, his signal for the midwife who lived on their land in a sharecropper's house.

When the midwife said it was a baby boy, Stella died peacefully. It was as if she had planned to leave Sonny with another farmhand while she chose to withdraw hers for a different place.

As he saw it, Stella would still be alive if he had let go of his promise to his father and heeded her plan to leave. Now, Sonny believed he also suffered the loss of his son James for his love of the land. He relentlessly withheld his blessing for James to join the navy and ultimately lost his youngest son to San Francisco. In his room covered in grief, Sonny was sure it was his fear of breaking the promise that drove James away. He had given James no out, putting the promise before his son's happiness. After enduring so much to hold on to the land, the death of another loved one was too much to bear.

CHAPTER THREE

*E*llie strolled from the barn into a sea of knee high brush. She had lingered for a few extra minutes of solitude after another Sunday liaison with Kent. She watched him heading home against a cloudless sky becoming a smaller and smaller dot, near motionless. Lightning bugs danced in the tall brown grass. Ellie tried to catch one as she took a different route home. She decided to bypass the farmhouse she had lived in with her mother and Mr. Spooky. It scared her. Those were dark years and part of Ellie's secret past lingered behind the worn and loose shingled house.

Night suddenly fell as Ellie cleared the trees, afraid of her own shadow. She heard her husband, Manny, calling her name. Ellie yelled back as she ran from the screams that she sometimes heard at night, ever since hearing the word "Chester" in his grandfather's will over a year ago.

Out of breath, she could see Manny rocking on the porch drinking from a glass. He sat cattycorner to the front white-painted, double-paneled doors. Insects prolonging their day gathered under the top light above his head between the wide columns.

When he saw her, Manny put aside his newspaper and toasted her with his drink. He quickly went inside and came out with two glasses. Manny met Ellie on the bottom step with a big kiss and lemon iced tea. She took her treat breathing hard.

"Hey, my cute track star," he smiled and pulled one of her ringlets.

It sprung back slipping from his fingers. After a year, Ellie hardly missed the straight hairstyles she wore in Chicago. Twisting had become a fashionable choice during the late nineties.

"Thanks for the great service," she said, breathing intensely between each word while taking the last porch step together with Manny.

He took her glass and sat it alongside his on a folding tray permanently placed by his rocking chair.

Manny confused Ellie's eagerness to reach him for happiness. He opened his arms for a hug saying, "Honey admit it, you're enjoying living on a farm again. The first year hasn't been half-bad." He tenderly squeezed her and kissed her neck. Rather than picking up his newspaper, he braced them for a two-step dance and joyfully said, "Once you get pregnant, things will be perfect."

On the wide porch, holding her waist, Manny dipped Ellie like they had learned in the ballroom dance classes as partners before becoming husband and wife three years ago.

"Wow," Ellie said when her head went back.

Standing her up, he situated one hand on her hair and fluffed her curls commenting, "See, you cut your long hair for nothing." Manny laughed, "And to think you protested like moving here was worse than the North Pole."

She joined in his laughter and slid away from his arms to the yellow faded ottoman next to Manny's rocking chair. Still grinning, he sat down and playfully massaged her tense shoulders.

Ellie had treaded cautiously through a very difficult year being back in Chester. Dividing her feelings between Kent and Manny was draining. It bothered her to make love to Manny, since the last man who touched her in Chester was Mr. Spooky. Ellie wrestled with how to assure Kent's forgiveness as she waited for the perfect chance to correct the biggest mistake that she made so many years ago. Even more anguishing, her nightmares were back. The screams were frequent. She would have to deal soon with secrets of the past for peace. Ellie was too tied up emotionally to become pregnant.

"You know I thought you were losing it when I told you we should leave Chicago for Chester," Manny haggled as he offered Ellie her half-full glass. Looking into her eyes he tapped his glass to hers. "Here, Here! To the next three years." He nodded with a big smile and took his last gulp. She held her glass chin level and grimaced before barely taking a sip.

***

When Manny announced the decision to move to Chester and farm the land, Ellie had protested. For three days, she had refused to get out of the bed. She cried whenever he entered the bedroom and pulled the Egyptian cotton covers over her head. The mostly yellow room with large windows had been her heaven, and she wanted it to stay that way. The night the will came, she had tossed and turned away from Manny's opened arms.

On cue most nights thereafter, Ellie woke up from nightmares of hearing the screams. The screams that she thought were left in Georgia after twenty years. Since the will arrived, Ellie had worried about her past during many restless nights.

Manny had attempted to pacify Ellie and kept a low profile. He intentionally avoided complaining about anything during those days. If the window blinds were closed and Manny wanted them open, he said nothing. When the toilet paper ran out, Manny searched high and low until he found some. He stepped lightly around the house, knowing that Ellie was not willing to move to Chester.

Her true inner conflict was invisible to Manny. Ellie chose to continue hiding her past and conceded she was losing the battle of staying in Chicago as she watched him ease in and out of the bedroom, smiling. On the fourth day, she went to his barbershop and because he prized her long permed hair, she cut it all off. The tension surrounding their move was solid, but she would not change his mind.

Soon after the last hair hit the floor, Manny's telephone rang in his Lakeshore Drive office. It was his private line. He whisked it up anticipating a fun break with Ellie.

"Hello, Manny speaking," he pushed the speakerphone button and leaned back, crossing his arms behind his head.

His Italian black suit jacket curled just perfectly in his lap. A fancy gold watch peeked from under his starched white shirt cuff, reflecting a prism from the sunlight shining through the office window. With his slightest arm movement, his expensive diamond dust cufflinks sparkled as he thought about his wife disliking their pending move.

"It's Joe, man," his barber said. "I've got some cruel news for you. I just cut all your wife's hair off."

The other end of the telephone was voiceless.

Joe hesitated, "Sorry man, but she demanded it."

"It's about going South," Manny indicated. "We'll work it out. Thanks for calling. I'll see you in a week for my cut," Manny added, looking at his wedding picture.

After work that day, Manny stepped in the marble foyer of their downtown condominium and yelled, "Honey! I'm home."

Ellie bounced out of the kitchen carrying a bottle of wine and two glasses. Dinner was cooked. He smelled lamb chops, his favorite. She expected and wanted Manny to fuss at the missing long curls. Rubbing one hand over her head, Ellie offered him a glass of Chardonnay to celebrate her deed. He took it. Her "new do" did not faze him.

Manny dropped his briefcase on a chair and held his arms wide holding the crystal stem with his fingertips.

"Come here, my love."

The classical music playing delicately inspired him to go for a warm hello kiss from his wife.

In the spring, like Manny decided, Ellie was moving back to Chester. Beaten like a heavyweight boxing champion blocking blows in a corner with no chance at winning, she stopped her stunts. Manny was a smart man. He would suspect Ellie was hiding something, if she did anything else out of character.

✳✳✳

To Ellie the last year had been bad. It was devastating for her from the very start. One year ago, Ellie managed to control her fears for a short while after hearing the news of moving back, until they hit the road that led into Chester. Everything was green or various shades of red dirt along the way into the tiny town. They saw some farmers' fields plowed, and where cows and horses fed in the rolling hay pastures. As they drove the two-lane highway large irrigation hoses occasionally sprayed their vehicle. Before they entered the city limits, a sign with three bullet holes read Chester three miles.

Ellie fought tears, her eyeballs hurt under the pressure of holding back the flood. She was seconds from being back, and she felt doomed. A familiar Sam Cooke tune played on the lone Black radio station they fought hard to locate. Surprisingly to Ellie and Manny, it blasted the oldies-but-goodies clear of static. Manny sang along, popping his thin fingers to the rocking beat as she fretted with what problems that awaited her in Chester.

Ellie concentrated on the passenger side of the roadway on open fields, houses, animals, big yellow combines and numerous red trailers. She recognized the area and a few old dilapidated houses sitting in fields behind worn fences. Ma Resta, bless her soul, Ellie thought, seeing the roof-sunken-in house where the peculiar lady had lived by herself with three pet squirrels and seven dogs.

Attempting to picture the hermit, Ellie could only remember the day the lady lay in the yard. She could see Ma Resta's feet with red and blue ringed socks. Ellie was five years old when she and her mama found her one Saturday unable to get up. Trying to recall what her mother's friend look liked, Ellie turned around in the roving vehicle as the familiar place moved out of sight.

Near the city limits, a graveyard had plenty of Confederate flags waving in the air even though the Memorial Day holiday was weeks away. Manny did not notice them. He posted his face straight ahead, oblivious to it all including Ellie's watery eyes.

Their Volvo entered the city limits of Chester as they drove slowly around the tiny City Hall Square. Ellie stared looking for anyone she knew, but hoping to see no one. Dogwood trees were fully bloomed and sported their many buds. The stench of fertilizer and swine cascaded in the air competing with sweet smelling fruit trees. The fire station, police department, and post office appeared all within arm's length of a single room behind one tiny door. In less than one minute they were leaving downtown and the city limits heading to the farm.

"That's it?" Manny complained.

Ellie nodded her head. She did not look at him.

Manny's last visit was when he was nineteen years old. The first year his grandfather wore the eye patch like a pirate. He had lost his eye the summer before, when Manny cancelled a planned visit to attend basketball camp during his senior year in high school. In his youth the place seemed larger.

Today the buildings appeared smaller. On his left, he saw the local hardware store. Across the square from it was a diner café under a pink and green awning, busy with people mingling. Feeling lost, Manny slowed the car and pulled into a roadside gas station.

"I don't know where we're going. It has been too long to remember," he said, intending to ask for directions.

Ellie remained uncomfortable and speechless.

When he was out of hearing distance she added, "I can probably get us to the Vinson's place and to where I used to live."

Ellie leaned her head with a few inches of new growth on the headrest feeling pitiful. She was worried about people recognizing and accusing her for what happened more than twenty years ago. Cutting her hair was meaningless. She had not changed much, only a little thicker wearing one-dress size up. Her escape would have been to quit Manny and never have returned. Coming back was a gamble.

Manny left the car motor running and his window down near a single-hose pump. Ellie smelled the freshness in the air in spite of the smelly gas. There was plenty of pollen in the air making her eyes burn. She sneezed three times. She watched Manny walk across the concrete slab, which aproned in front of the building where a tall man exited asking, "Can I help you?"

The gas attendant met Manny halfway ready to provide full service. He wore striped overalls with a dirty red handkerchief hanging out of his chest pocket. He fanned plenty of gnats as he talked with Manny, never treating him as a stranger. Ellie heard the attendant with a curled up mustache cackle at Manny being a newcomer.

"I can handle it now." Manny returned putting one long leg in the car. He mistakenly blew his horn climbing in, but continued, "He said to go pass two more hard roads, veer left, and continue until we see a big church with a steeple. Then we take a left straight to my grandfather's farmhouse." Manny made himself comfortable in the driver's seat and winked at Ellie.

"Let's go. It's five o'clock." Ellie checked the car's digital clock, worrying about what was going to happen soon. It was just a matter of time and she knew it. "These backwoods can be pretty dark. City lights are a joke here," Ellie muttered as they pulled on the rock and gravel road.

"I had the lights turned on, Babe." Manny glanced at a giant mulberry tree.

"For both of the houses or just one?" Ellie interjected.

"That's a good question. I'm not sure." He pressed the automatic button, rolling up his window. They drove on.

"I remember this," Ellie pointed.

They turned at the big church and Manny continued driving to what felt like a pot of gold at the end of a rainbow.

"Is this the way to your old house?" he asked.

"Yep," Ellie quipped and hurriedly sat up to pay closer attention to where they were going.

Ellie's eyes grew bigger as she recognized the church. The scenery was exactly like she remembered from years ago. An old rock and stone well with a wooden roof sat off the road. The pine trees that sheltered her favorite hideaway as a child were lined up like green uniformed soldiers standing at attention in the distance. Behind them, stood Ellie's and Kent's abandoned barn. They passed the way to the Vinson's place. Their land was along the right side of the roadway. On the other side was Mr. Spooky's land.

Not a chance in hell, Ellie thought. She began coughing drowning out the radio. She put her hands over her mouth and turned away from Manny. Bending her head forward to her lap with steady coughs, Ellie's breathing grew progressively erratic with each new one.

"What's the matter?" Manny said, reaching over to pat her on the back.

Ellie coughed uncontrollably, unable to speak. She held her neck and appeared to be choking. Manny abruptly stopped the car to console her.

"Are you going to be alright?" he asked.

Ellie panicked. Her body twisted with fear that Manny's grandfather's house was her old house. They had a short distance to complete their journey. Several feet ahead on the left would be a dead end dirt road leading to Mr. Spooky's.

"Honey, I think we're almost there. Can you hold on?" Manny applied the gas, drove a few feet and turned left.

"Dead End" was hand painted on a metal sign. The car moved forward, taking Ellie to a place that she hated. A huge wood and shingle house was mounted at the end of the car lights. Manny veered into a makeshift driveway defined by patches of dirt between overgrown centipede grass. The shrubbery, a mixture of boxwoods and spicebushes, was wild and in need of major pruning. The house appeared dark and dreary except for hundreds of early blooming white miniature roses that spilled over onto the wraparound porch.

"We're here," Manny said and jumped out of the car circling it to assist Ellie.

Her breasts climbed higher and higher with each new breath. Manny reached into the backseat and brought out bottled water from a cooler, holding Ellie into his chest. He glided back to a stoop at the passenger's side door.

"Here Ellie, take a drink." He guided the bottle to his wife's mouth and rubbed her back.

She wrapped her hands around his, cupping the bottle. She drank hard and fast, glancing at the terrifying sight. "You can take a look inside. I'll wait here," Ellie gestured that she was OK, but she was not.

Manny agreed and headed for the raggedy house.

"It doesn't look good from here," she hollered as he walked the doorsteps. "Be careful, it might collapse."

Ellie turned her head away from the house. She had witnessed its horror. It was too painful and she never wanted to set foot in that house. Ellie would leave Manny before she lived there again.

When Manny was out of sight. She heard screams. Ellie closed both car doors. Hers first and with a long reach she closed Manny's in an almost reflex action. She trembled as she hit the automatic door lock and clutched her ears.

Ellie did not see this coming. She had worried about Kent not forgiving her deeds and having to face the reason she left for Chicago. But the chance that a single house of a hundred in this tiny one-horse town would be willed to them by Mr. Spooky shattered her. How could this be? Was Mr. Spooky alive all those years?

She had left him for dead some twenty years ago and escaped to Chicago to avoid any charges. Her tears flowed mercilessly.

Ellie slumped over in her seat overwhelmed with confusion. She could have stayed in Chester—married Kent and had his child. But Ellie had assumed Mr. Spooky was dead and fled. If he was Manny's grandfather, she had run away for nothing.

The screams continued louder. Was it her mother's cry for help, or Mr. Spooky whom she had left splattered in a pool of blood still haunting her? He took away her mother, her lover and her child. Would he now take away Manny?

Ellie heard something knocking on the car. It scared her. She jumped bracing her hands and digging her nails in the dashboard. The sound was louder. She closed her eyes and yelled at the top of her lungs.

"Let me in!" It was Manny banging on the driver's side window.

He beat harder.

Ellie's wide eyes met Manny's. He stretched his arms full length and hunched his shoulders. She pressed the unlocked button with nervous fingers. Manny snapped the door opened and quickly sat down.

"What are you screaming for?" he asked.

Ellie remained quiet.

"The house is a mess inside. Let's see what the other one looks like." He was disappointed.

They backed up and drove another half a mile on a narrow dirt road. A trail of dust puttered behind the Volvo, which rolled in and out of potholes. Trees lined their path of tough weeds that scraped the sides of the car. Suddenly, on the right, they faced a stately red brick two story with columns gracing a wide front porch. The lights were not juiced.

Manny looked at Ellie and asked, "Where to now?"

She was thinking anywhere but Mr. Spooky's house.

CHAPTER FOUR

*N*ine months eagerly swam the river of time since the day James was buried. In June of 1998, Sonny continued to openly grieve long after the crowds in mourning black had marched out of the funeral recessional two by two. Sonny appeared delicate and diminutive in the all-dark garbs, which he wore as self-punishment like ladies who lost their husbands at war. Losing a child who was supposed to bury you took his spirit about everything, including the land.

On the eve of his seventy-ninth birthday, Sonny's days were still preoccupied with his loss of James and what to do about the life-stealing farm. Haunted by his covenant with the land, Sonny had given out. The pain of losing his youngest son tore at the fabric of keeping his promise. Frail and old, he was ready to give up weaving the burden into the tapestry of his last days.

Sonny had lived a full life bearing the commitment to farm the land. For too long, he had watched Kent toiling relentlessly with the soil and began to wonder if it was worth it. To be faithful on his promise, Sonny needed Kent to produce an heir for the land. Now an old man, he would not be around forever as Father Time slowly was claiming his strength.

Searching for an answer, he saw the possibility of failing on his promise since losing one son, and he grappled with what to do. With the memory of James gashing at his soul and tearing him further down into mere existence, Sonny pondered whether his last son should spend more time on the farm. Surely, Kent was breathing the dust and bearing the daily duties to keep what Sonny now realized would also be his doom.

Kent was Sonny's only heir to the land, and he knew nothing of the burden. Sonny knew if something happened to Kent, the land would be lost in the deal made more than fifty years ago to save his life. Should the torch of the Moccasin Pond deal pass to Kent to save the land?

At forty, Kent should have been married with kids of his own, but the land had a way of grabbing hold of a farmer's life until days turned into years, and years into decades, and decades into forever. Although he felt strongly about keeping his land and legacy of farming, Sonny could not let Kent be like him in another ten years, wondering if he should have been somewhere else other than the farm. In a larger town, Kent could find a wife, marry and have a family. He knew in his heart that it was time to let Kent go.

Sonny had tried to hold on to Stella. Keeping the promise, he had lost her. After almost a year, his peace still eluded him for holding on to James, just to lose him also because of the promise.

Under the strain of grief, Sonny had determined Kent's leaving would serve the land more than his daily duties of plowing, planting, and feeding cattle. Sonny saw clearly that he had given up too much holding onto the farm. Ultimately, his only way to keep his promise was letting Kent part with the land. Today, he would ask him to leave.

At 5:00 p.m., Kent usually came home to fix supper. He had fallen into a daily routine of getting up at 5:00 a.m. to cook breakfast for Sonny and fix lunch for the both of them. Each morning, he fed his dad hot oatmeal with toast. He put lunch consisting of meat, one vegetable and bread in the oven. To preserve his time working, Kent would take a sacked sandwich to work in the fields. He would come in at five o'clock when he turned over the plowing to his hired help. Being with his dad was important to him since his brother's death. He understood that life was short and precious, so every moment he spent with Sonny, Kent counted as blessed.

Coming in from the field to continue his house chores, Kent was dusty from head to toe. A wide straw hat he wore to shield the sun was sour with a large wet ring. His yellow shirt appeared spotted black from an oil spill while refueling the tractor at noon. Working through lunch was a way to finish planting an early crop, which was sometimes necessary to pay loans called due sooner than expected. Farming was like a crap game—you had to beat time to win. Constantly under the threat of weather conditions, many crops were sown too soon and spoil. Whole fields fried to mere weeds when the rain was slow. Each season, another Prince Hall Mason brother fell from the ranks, losing his land.

Calling it a day and quitting on time, Kent headed home. Pausing at the backdoor, he slipped his left boot off. It landed on the bottom step. While holding the door ajar, the other rolled onto the grass when he stuck his right boot heel against a step and pressed hard. His white socks were mostly red from where the plowed dirt seeped into his shoes' eyes and tongues. He was tired with an aching back.

Kent considered hiring a cook, but he remembered the days when money was tight. He had held a job working at a tire factory forty miles away to make ends meet. He did the mindless work for nearly twenty years saving and earning a nice pension while having full responsibilities on the farm. His fulltime job had saved their land from foreclosure three times. Times had been hard. Sonny had borrowed from the bank to pay the government and vice versa, depending on which was breathing the hardest on his neck.

"Daddy, how you doing?" Kent yelled when he cleared the door threshold.

"Just fine son, but we need to talk."

"Can I wash up and start supper?" Kent asked, testing the emotions behind his father's statement.

Whatever it was, Kent sensed it was important.

Sonny nodded as he sat at the kitchen table, waiting to speak. Listening to the five-o-clock news, he pressed his hand mindlessly over the flowered tablecloth circling the blue pansies one at a time. Heavy cast iron pots hung over the stove, reflecting the last bit of the sunlight. The appliances were shiny white. Part of Sonny's uneaten lunch sat on top of the stove in a covered tin pan. On the refrigerator was a blue magnet with the Bible verse Philippians 4:13.

Kent hoped his father had not seen his care and love for the farm fading. He left the kitchen marching into the guest bathroom, which was his designated space. The men had divided up the extra rooms, making one an office and using the other for entertainment. Since James's death, Sonny had moped around aimlessly in the house they all once shared, seeing James in every room.

While showering, Kent rehearsed an excuse for Sonny, anticipating a verbal lashing from his father about slacking in his work. His daily steady routine was done to keep busy and his mind off James and Ellie. Like a robot, Kent cooked while Sonny gave him an update on the evening news. Sonny recanted a detailed account of the local station's theft and assaults between a series of "It-ain't-like-it-use-to-be's." He peppered the story of an escaped prisoner with his long conservative commentary as Kent stirred to set the table.

"How in the world does a man think he can hide from the law?" he said to Kent in a matter-of-fact way. Sonny shook his head. "I want my freedom. That rascal had a life sentence for killing somebody." Sonny spilled as he over talked The Wheel of Fortune.

"Uh huh," Kent mumbled so his dad would know that he was listening.

"Where could he go and be free? Just tell me." Sonny questioned the air. "He sold his God given freedom for a few pennies. It's just a shame what happens these days." Sonny chewed out the TV report as Kent agreed to every word he said.

Before sunset, they graced a table of green beans, pork chops and buttered rice. Kent lifted his first spoonful.

"Son, you have my blessings to leave this place." Sonny began their talk.

Chewing fast to respond, Kent watched as Sonny cut a piece of pork chop and pierced it with a fork.

"Dad, what are you talking about?" he said, getting annoyed with the suggestion as he finished swallowing.

"Well, Son, if something happens to you we'll lose the farm," Sonny choked out the words.

"I know you haven't gotten over James. You shouldn't worry about such things," Kent pleaded.

"Kent, you deserve your own family and children. Don't you want that for yourself?" Sonny asked and went into a twenty-minute speech on the birds and the bees as Kent rolled his eyes but listened.

"Sure, it'll happen when it's time," Kent offered.

"Son, I thought if you moved to a larger town you might find a wife. I know there are women here, but you don't seem interested except for that little teacher, and I haven't heard a word about her since Ellie returned," Sonny said a little agitated.

"Dad, you can stop this nonsense. OK," Kent demanded. Tired after a full day's work, he got up from his ladder-back chair, clearing the table.

Chewing his last bite of food, Sonny pushed his plate about six inches away from him, scooted his chair back and crossed his legs.

They both hushed.

Minutes passed with Kent washing the dishes and getting concerned about his father, before he asked, "Did you take your high blood pressure pill? You're a little riled." With suds on his hands, he pointed to the cabinet for Sonny to take his pill.

"It's time I tell you what has been the devil about this property for more than fifty years," Sonny snapped. "Get your wallet and keys. I'll take you there," he said, upset.

Kent did not have the energy to fight with Sonny, so he did what he was told.

They drove for thirty minutes out of their county to a smaller town for Sonny's show-and-tell in the swamps. Both were silent during the drive except for when Sonny gave directions. Kent was mesmerized that his dad was really serious. Seeing the stiff profile of his father, Kent was thinking that he could marry tomorrow, if Sonny would ease up on this devil business.

Almost there, Sonny pointed ahead and stated, "Once we round this bend, take the first road on the right, drive until you see a pond and park. Don't go too close to the bank, alright?" He stopped pointing and in a forced voice, said, "Be sure to stop where it's clear. There are snakes in the pond."

Tree limps reached over the tiny vine-tangled lane as they trucked along. The grooves in the narrow path were overgrown indicating that no one had been there for years. Tall weeds splashed on the front of the truck's hood and scrubbed the bottom, which made a constant thrashing sound and unnerved Kent. As they drove further on the bumpy lane, it grew darker and the sky vanished under the thick, wide low bearing trees in the swamp. Sounds unknown played tricks on their ears. Some yapped, others whooped, it was foreboding. Only something terrible could be there. Suddenly, they reached a clearing where the dimmed evening sky reopened over a murky pond.

"This place is hard to find. How do you know about it?" Kent spoke as he pulled up the brake clutch, stopping in sight of black shallow water.

"If you were in trouble, you would know, son. That's why we're here. It was 1944." Sonny began to tell the story.

***

A new model Ford had recently debuted. It was a rare sight. One could hear it chugging and get excited at the sound of the engine.

Sonny chuckled recalling the memory. "Your grandfather was a gambling man in his heart—almost anywhere and anybody willing, if the deal was a true deal. He was smart about his choices and as fair as he could be." Sonny eyed the deadly pond. He sighed at the situation he faced. "A good gambling deal made my daddy's soul get happy. He was known to honor them. It came close to costing us the land a few times." Sonny sat in the truck observing an area where plenty of folk had disappeared.

One day over fifty years ago, Sonny's father came home with a brand spanking new Ford that he had won fairly in a few towns over from Chester. A black man was not supposed to have a nice car, no matter where he lived. The news spread like butter in the hot sun throughout the five county areas and over the entire swamp.

Telling the story, Sonny got out of the truck at the familiar sight that faced him that dreadful day. He spoke as Kent joined him in a safe spot.

"Well, son," Sonny breathed exhaustedly and picked up a stick. "At the time, I was twenty-five years old. Anytime we drove that car folk stood like statues and watched. I was on my way to purchase a new trailer to haul peanuts, when my life changed. I mistakenly hit a white lady," he said somberly.

The attention of the fancy car fell sour when Sonny hit the elderly lady crossing in the middle of the street on a foggy day. He was in the next county, and there was not a familiar face around.

A gang had enfolded the vehicle before he could get out. They pulled him from the sleek ride and shoved Sonny onto the ground. His shoulders and elbows scraped the pavement hard. His wounds were not so bloody, because Sonny jumped with the movement, breaking his impact.

Sonny was defenseless in the time before rights were civil. He had pleaded that it was an accident, but the vigilante crowd did not listen. One of them hastily pulled a shotgun from the rear window of a truck. Sonny soon saw eight white faces and two-barrel holes staring at him as he peered up, frightened to pieces at the gun pointed to his face. Sonny was about to lose his life.

Sonny seemed weaker recalling the scene. "I felt the butt of the shotgun crash against my skull and the world went black. When I woke up they had brought me here to Moccasin Pond in the swamp after taking the car keys and putting me in a flatbed wagon." Sonny trembled reliving his fear as he watched the space around his feet. Sonny swallowed hard, "Son, no one ever lived to come out of the pond."

Hundreds of moccasins bred in the murk. Black heads with big dark eyes bobbed like stomps. That terrible night Sonny had awakened with a splitting headache to rustling movement on the bank of the pond.

Suddenly, one shot rang through the swamp, blasting minutes after it was fired to settle the crowd. Everyone hushed. Their attention was on Sonny and a man named Sprewell who had pulled the trigger. He said the Ford was his car lost in a late night poker game with Pope Vinson, Sonny's father, and he was determined to win it back. Sprewell declared it was his battle not theirs.

He announced through checkered teeth that the "old battle-axe" was up walking, when he heard of the incident and rushed to Moccasin Pond.

"Y'all can go home; the lady is fine," he ordered with his gun held like he was ready to shoot.

Sonny laid flat on his back listening to the slithering and splashing snakes in the pond. Angry men with guns and a rope had Sonny at death's doorstep. He was resigned to never seeing his family again. He was as good as dead and knew it. Missing his shoes with the shirt torn off his left arm, Sonny had heard many stories about Moccasin Pond and of lives lost there. He had gotten himself in a world of trouble with these angry white men.

"Alright, I ain't telling y'all again," Sprewell said to the eight men and the rest of the crowd. "You hot heads can cool down or answer to the law. I mean it," he shouted aggressively.

After holding their ground for a few minutes, the crowd stirred. Then the instigator spat tobacco, nodded to the others, and called the man who had fired the gun, "Sheriff Sprewell."

Resisting, the ringleader had mumbled that they should kill him anyway for showboating around their town in a brand new car. Looking for support, he checked the faces of the others. They had their hands in their pockets, stepping backward.

About ten feet from the pond, Sonny saw the men clearing back as snakes were lurking a few feet away. Then his eyes glued on the man who held the gun as smoke swirled from its mouth. And white faded gradually against the night.

Sonny wanted to live and the guy who was calling off the posse was his best ticket out of Moccasin Pond. He hung on the sheriff's words wanting to live. Sheriff Sprewell spoke with authority that he was taking Sonny back to his cheating daddy. His words gave Sonny hope of seeing daylight to live again.

Sonny scrambled to his knees.

"I can't afford no more trouble like this." Sheriff Sprewell chastised the last man who did not want to listen to him—his blood brother. "If one more suspicious thing happens in this county the righteous crew will have my head," he grumbled with disappointment that he had to answer to others.

They had reluctantly backed off like cowboys in a western movie making a bank robbery getaway, checking the tellers until they reached the door.

"I'm on y'all's side, but my back is against the wall this time. It's too much, too soon since the last one," he scolded. Staring down his brother, Sprewell shouted, "I can't explain every missing person away!" He shook his head, hating to let his crowd down.

The swamp noises sang as the once revved up men were diffused from their deed and returned grudgingly to their rides. With a rebel flag flying, they pulled out, hollering like they had won a football game.

It was like it was yesterday for Sonny, standing there sweating as he continued. "I then found myself standing before Sprewell, the man who had owned the car. I quickly offered it back to him, but he told me my life was worth more than one car. He said mad as fire. 'What about all your daddy's land? That's a better deal,' he smacked while holding the gun on me. I tried to answer, but before I could he kicked me in the ribs."

Sonny had fallen to the ground, watching a moccasin in the water glide to the edge, when he rustled up in pain. Bleeding from the mouth and with a massive headache, Sprewell took him to his father, and the deal was done.

Sonny's young life was traded for the farmland. Sheriff Sprewell offered the deal to Pope Vinson who respected it as fair under the circumstances. He had lost a few unlucky acquaintances to Moccasin Pond.

Unfortunately, his bad habit had put Sonny at risk, but he felt obligated, since his gambling partner's actions had also saved his son's life. The two gamblers shook hands on a deal that if the land was ever sold out of the Vinson's family, it had to be to the Sprewells. If there were no next of kin in the line of Vinsons, the Sprewells stood in the shoes of the Vinsons just like any family heir. They would take the land free and clear. Sprewell put it on paper and Pope Vinson signed it.

Sonny ended the story saying, "I first said forget Sprewell, but he made me promise that I wouldn't go back on his word. I took the blame for that day, so I promised my daddy that the deal would never be. He'd signed away part of his honor. Your granddaddy was an honorable man like many others who back in the times didn't have much choice in being tricked out their land to protect life. Knowing how he felt, I swore that I would keep the land in our family no matter what it took. I'm partly at fault, and I do this on his word, only."

Sonny had been true to his promise.

***

Sonny looked at his son as he finished the story. The memory took a lot out of him. He was weary because his life was the reason the land was put on the line. Sonny wanted Kent to see that they were the only two possible heirs to the Vinsons land. Sonny had outlived his only brother by fifteen years, whose wife was unable to bear children. Between the two of them, Kent was the only one who could produce another heir. Now, Kent knew about the Moccasin Pond deal, and ultimately the burden was on his shoulders.

"See, you need a wife and some kids. I could die in peace knowing that the next generation would make my daddy proud," Sonny said, with a dry mouth from telling the burden he had carried most of his life.

"Dad, you've been a rock," Kent said and put his hand around his father's shoulder as he seethed about the nerve of some people.

"Son, I get a visit every year from the Sprewells to remind me of the pact we made all those years ago. First it was the senior Sprewell. He passed the deal in writing and the mark that my father made on his makeshift contract to his children. Now Sprewell Jr., about my age, is trying to outlive me for this land," Sonny said, knowing that he must impress upon Kent the urgency to do something soon.

"I see more than I ever have about your commitment to the farm. I'm sorry it was so tragic. You've been through so much," Kent said, worrying about the future.

"I guess you'll get the visit one day, when I'm gone," Sonny added, ready to head back home. The splashing snakes were beginning to bother him.

To lighten up their visit to Moccasin Pond, Kent pointed and yelled jokingly, "I see one!"

Sonny, slightly jumpy, kicked his heels, high-stepping to avoid any of the deadly moving creatures.

"Just kidding," Kent laughed.

"Son, I know I threw this on you suddenly, but think about it. On the other hand, we could probably rent the land out to Ellie's husband. I think his name is Manny.

Uh huh, he knows what he's doing now, with plenty of good help," Sonny said, thinking already about a Plan B.

"Don't bother." Kent waved off his dad's statement.

They climbed into the truck and traced their route from Moccasin Pond. On the way across the county, Kent decided to ask Minnie Jean, the schoolteacher he once courted, to marry him. This would please his father.

On the road near home, a car passed them traveling too fast for the narrow roadway. It was Ellie. The Vinsons waved, and Kent tooted the horn. Her vehicle hummed and flashed by them like a streak of black. She was on a mission heading farther toward Mr. Spooky's old house.

CHAPTER FIVE

Ellie rushed the car into Mr. Spooky's old yard running over a bed of blooming tiger lilies. Her library books jolted to the floor before the engine sputtered to silence. She sat in the dark for fifteen minutes, holding the steering wheel. Having teased the whole day with her on-again-off-again decision to make peace with the screams, Ellie was tormented. She finally garnered the nerve, switching the ignition back on. She turned on the car's bright lights aimed at the front of the dark house.

Under her eyes were circles from sleepless nights full of screams. She was losing weight and shedding hair. Manny had begun to ask too many questions, and Ellie was sure he was suspicious. Inside the broken down house, she could face her past with Mr. Spooky and her mother. Tonight, she had to do it and do it now.

Ellie got out where a lamp post beamed a soft light, but she could see no more than a few feet to the back of the car. Using the bright headlights, she would have to be brave enough to reach the door and find the light switch.

Mounting the dirt walkway, she was dressed in a purple warm-up and black tennis shoes. She wore a colorful paisley print scarf tied around her head. Her bangs spilled from the top of her crown, making a firework of loose hairs.

Focusing on the front door, Ellie pressed on. The first doorstep squeaked as she placed her right foot down. She heard an owl whoo loudly, and chills shot up her spine. She gathered her bearings as crickets sang the sounds she remembered loving as a little girl.

The next step creaked and partially gave in. Sinking, she ran up the last three steps and landed on all fours. Large holes were in the porch. A weathered rocker, missing a leg and most of its caning, was leaning against the side of the house under a large picture window facing the yard. The railings of the wraparound porch were checkered like the teeth of a seven-year-old, and the screen door was ripped off. The faded gray wide shingles appeared dreary like they were when she had lived there. Building up more confidence, Ellie stood up walking through heavy threads of spider webs and twisted the doorknob.

She opened the door pushing it forward. Holding her breath, she placed her sweaty palm inside and located the familiar light switch. She pushed. Nothing happened. Ellie spread her fingers wider searching for a second switch and flipped it. A five-bulb chandelier with two working bulbs lit up the room, and an old house smell hit her nose. The air was musty and stale.

Inside, she was there where Mr. Spooky had made her mother, Claudine, cry and scream all night when Ellie was sixteen. Her stomach churned reliving the scene, which was noisy with lots of fussing. Her mother and Mr. Spooky had bantered back and forward most of the morning, until he went late to the fields. But before supper, the pop-eyed man returned cussing as he came in walking heavily.

He had been angry for two days since several guys in town whistled at her mother wearing an all white outfit, a wide brim hat and her gold chain necklace with her initial "C" on it. When Claudine said it was boys being boys, he slapped her mouth. The sound was powerful. Her front tooth popped out and flew across the room, leaving Claudine's lips red. She bled and the house was noisy again.

As a reflex, Ellie had scampered to the floor to retrieve the tooth. Mr. Spooky, demanding respect, took one rough crackled-skin hand and squeezed her neck. His force stood her up. Turning pink under the pressure, she held her breath until he released her. Following a tongue-lashing she would never forget, Ellie had crashed to the hard floor, fearing for her and her mother's life.

Near the fireplace, she saw the area of the bloodstains, a gush from the tooth torn from its roots, and where he had dragged her mother into the master bedroom, making a spotted red trail. She recalled Mr. Spooky making her wipe and clean the blood until he was satisfied. Three hours later, he ordered her to bed. Ellie's eyes followed the path as she remembered the horror. The stains, darkened with age, were still visible, but her sad memories were vivid. Being there was hypnotizing.

"Mother, mother!" Ellie cut the musty silence in the house she ran out of in shock as a seventeen-year-old girl. "I'm so sorry I didn't do anything to stop him. I was scared." She cried with tears streaming along her puffy cheeks.

Ellie crumpled the front of her purple top as she testified to the walls and begged for forgiveness. Her wrinkle-free fabric churned like butter under the constant wringing and unconscious twisting of her hands.

"Forgive me, forgive me," Ellie paraded in circles stomping. "Mama, I heard you calling for help. You poor soul screamed and screamed." She could hear the same screams like that night, which now breathed a life of their own, fueling her guilt. "I was so tired from bending and wiping. I heard you screaming."

Her pleading traveled into the stale air.

"I'm so sorry, so sorry, I didn't help," Ellie echoed. Doubled over at the waist to bear the pain, she cried, "When I woke up in the morning, the screaming was gone." She said, louder, "You were gone."

The house vibrated with Ellie's stomping as she continued to call out to the walls for forgiveness. To her not much had changed except the dusty white sheets covering pieces of furniture arranged in front of the fireplace. The same picture of the Last Supper hung on the wall above the mantel. The wall paint peeled in patches on all four sides. The top layer of white gave way to a light blue in some spaces and heavy puke green in others. Blue was there when she left. And her mother's Holy Bible sat in the middle of the spindle leg coffee table.

Ellie's eyes careened over the ugly scene of Mr. Spooky and her mother. Staggering up, she ripped a sheet from a chair as her voice suddenly changed into a quiver. Then heavy anger rose up through her body. Her tears trickled dry like a stream in a desert drought, and it was quiet. Ellie stood motionless as her eyes darted about.

Then in the loudest, meanest tone she could muster, Ellie exploded, "Why did you leave without me?"

Turning a steady rhythm left and right, she pleaded, "Where did you go? Why couldn't I find you?"

Her arms flopped like wings of a bird rushing South for winter as she flung her body into a wall and slid down next to the wooden oven.

"It was not right to leave me here!" Ellie shouted, feeling the years of pain. "Where are you? You could've come back for me!"

She had come seeking forgiveness from her mother, but it was anger she felt. Her cries leveled to moaning as she let go a ton of hurt she had carried since the night of her mother's screams. Completely exhausted, her mouth opened to cascading little groans.

She remembered the next morning Mr. Spooky was equally surprised that Claudine was not there fixing their breakfast. The rooster cock-a-doodled early, but Ellie had stayed in bed, hoping a truce was made during the night.

His heavy knocking pounded on her door splitting the peace. The doorknob twisted and his bulging eyes had stared at her when he asked her where was Claudine. Ellie had leaped from bed running from room to room yelling, "Mama!"

When she had circled in the last one, it was evident the two were alone, and she blamed herself for not protecting her mother that night.

Now, Ellie was angry they had moved in with a man twice her mother's age. She realized Mr. Spooky had treated them so recklessly because they had allowed him. Reeling from her revelation, Ellie resolved it had not been her fault that her mother left. She could have done nothing to help that night, but only leave as her mother had.

But leaving Chester was a mistake as Ellie thought of Kent. She knew he could not understand her leaving, since she had not understood herself, until this very night.

The day Ellie left Chester, she was devoted to him, but to save herself she broke his heart. And like heaving dirt on a grave, she had buried their dreams of being together when she hid the fact she had left Mr. Spooky for dead.

After twenty years of running for her freedom, Ellie was relieved to learn her first day back in Chester that the mean old man had lived. She was clear with the law, but her haunting secret had been in vain.

The house bore witness to her act of self-defense. The fireplace near the wood burning stove was where she had thrown the piece of firewood. She had held it high ready to strike, begging Mr. Spooky to leave her alone. She had been in his house close to a year without her mother ducking and dodging his orders, hoping her mother would come soon.

On the day she fled, Ellie had been excited preparing for her wedding, which was three days away. She laid out her white wedding dress and fiddled with her hair. She pranced around her room imagining life with Kent. Ellie had forgotten about the daily duties of fixing Mr. Spooky's supper by the evening news. Lately, she had been sleepy and drained.

Before nightfall, Mr. Spooky came home steaming when he saw the pots empty. He made her start cooking immediately. Ellie worked quickly rattling pots to hurry supper under his evil stares. With trembling hands, she was moving as fast as she could, and dropped a slab of meat on the floor.

Mr. Spooky was furious and hounded her with verbal abuses of his disapproval of the wedding. He wanted her there as his help, not his neighbor's. Worse, losing Ellie reminded him of losing her mother who had outwitted him to freedom. Getting madder at her carelessness, he moved toward Ellie with arms swinging wide to strike. She dodged him and grabbed a piece of wood stacked beside the hot wood burning stove. A second swing, he caught her arm but she ripped free. Rushing in on her, Mr. Spooky missed again, lost his balance, and fell onto the stove, hitting his eye on a sharp corner. It shot blood.

Ellie had flinched when it splattered on her. He was screaming and groaning. Hearing him, she was paralyzed with the memory of her mother when Claudine was down on the floor bleeding, and Mr. Spooky had not allowed her to help. Thrashing on the floor, he spread the streaming flood from his face. Breathing hard, thinking about her mother, Ellie leaned over him and after a while his movement ceased. She had walked away terrified that he was dead.

In her room, she took off her clothes, washed, and put on her best dress—her wedding dress that she would not wear on the day she had lived for—to marry Kent. She maneuvered in slow motion shocked. When she had finished dressing, she walked to Mr. Spooky lying on the floor. She stepped over him with her new matching dyed shoes afraid he was stone cold. Ellie did not know what to do or where she was going. She had backed away hurriedly out of the door, striding until she reached Kent's house.

He was delighted to see her so pretty and dressed up. They stole away to the barn. And she left him the next day for Chicago.

Ellie never set foot into Mr. Spooky's house again, until now. She had waited in the train station all night for the next train north, which was Chicago. She escaped with fear and guilt. Now, she realized it was not her fault, that the old man had hurt himself that terrifying day.

She had to make sense of her life. Touching the wooden stove, Ellie released the bottled up fear that she had killed Mr. Spooky. She took a deep breath, knowing her life was spinning out of control. Since returning to Chester, her husband was living with a different person. There in the house full of sad memories she forgave herself for walking away. It was time she lived with peace in Chester. Ellie wanted the screams to stop.

Ellie pointed forcefully at the bloodstains shouting, "You lost an eye old man! I lost my mother!"

She shuddered at the thought that he wore an eye patch and was good as new, when she lived all those years thinking she had killed him.

Ellie's word "mother" suspended the air and rang in her ears through the silence. She held her arms out mumbling to the memory, "Oh my baby, my child." She beat her hands against the wall and pressed her face to it crying, "You ruined everything for me, my home, my child. All because of you old man." She pouted. "Because of you..." Weary and tired she demanded, "We're even, you hear! Please, leave me alone!"

Ellie wept uncontrollably, beating on the stove. Coughing in the disturbed dust, she spat, "I gave my child away."

Ellie had lost her soul when the little baby girl left her arms. She was a mother of a twenty-two-year-old daughter somewhere beyond Mr. Spooky's doors. It was her fault that she gave up her child for adoption after giving birth in Chicago. With this one big secret she would leave with little peace.

***

Beginning to worry about Ellie, Manny checked his watch, it was 10 p.m. It was Friday night, and he suspected the worse. When he came in from buying steers, her car was gone. He knew Ellie had not made friends with anyone since her return. She only regularly went to the library for books. But there were her Sunday walks after dinner when she was anxious to get out of the house by 3:30, otherwise Ellie was always home when he had returned in the evenings from working.

With her gone at this late hour, he began to think it quite strange that Ellie had never asked him to accompany her walks. A few times she had shunned his suggestion to join her. Where was she going? What was she doing?

Manny huffed, "She doesn't need to lose weight."

Since arriving in Chester, Ellie had lost ten pounds. He knew she had to be kidding him the walks were for her girlish figure. She was way too skinny, and something was amiss.

Manny had overheard some cheap shots and rumblings of his farmhands talking under their breaths about Ellie and a man no one would name. The usual town gossip was nonsense to him and he rarely listened. He had shoved any talk about Ellie off as jealousy.

Intentionally, Manny stayed out of the fray of the gossips except when he went digging up facts to hire good and reliable help. His best helpers were referrals, outright requests for work, and from overhearing who unfortunately had lost their land.

Hearing about Zachary Glasser's loss was a classic example of the good in the community among the busybodies. Manny had pursued and interviewed him for the last job opening three months ago.

Wanting to hire Zachary, Manny showed up early one morning only to face a "Keep Out" sign posted across their property entrance. Looking for the young man, he stopped for coffee at the café where Tall Nancy filled him in with the sad details. Zachary's father had lost their land after having it in the family for more than one hundred years. The loans had swallowed him whole.

The years of yielding bumper crops of soybeans, peanuts and vegetables he sold through the cooperative could not save him. All the times of managing with minimum cash and supplies were not enough to save him from trickery. His family and helpers stuck loyally beside him working seven days a week to prevent crops from spoiling in the fields. But in the end, nothing that he had controlled caused him to fail. It was the system around his loans that snuffed his dreams. Borrowing a little bit had cost him a lot—every acre of land, a brick house and farming equipment down to the last bent up old trailer.

With the plug pulled on their means for making a living, things dominoed and Zachary's father, a faithful farmer, was shut out of the house he had lived in since birth. Their house was boarded up. Locked out of the only home they ever had the Glasser family became disillusioned.

The young man Manny was looking for had been back from college for one year, ready to follow in his father's footsteps. He had turned down a job with a computer company in Atlanta to do what he really loved. After the foreclosure, the poor young fellow broke into the house to gather their most personal belongings. The Glassers were farmers one day and homeless the next. Pride drove his father to leave town and live with his brother in New Orleans in a one-room apartment. Zachary watched him carry his few items in a brown paper bag like a Santa's tummy on a bus, which took away his father who had lost all hope.

Tall Nancy played a tune for the newest farmer in town giving him an earful of grief about the Glassers. When Manny interrupted her for the third time to ask the simple question of where he could find Zachary, she mentioned in a roundabout way that his mother had a mental breakdown and moved into the nursing home way before her time.

After paying his tab, Manny did not seem any closer to finding Zachary than when he ordered the brown mug of coffee, alongside a counter full of regulars. Then Tall Nancy added that Zachary went to see his mother everyday at noon, and he was looking for work.

Zachary was highly qualified to do farm work. He had spent all of his life on his family farm until attending Morehouse College. Manny knew Zachary was a good choice to mentor for managing the Clayton's property once he and Ellie left in three years.

On that day at noon, Manny wandered the halls of the nursing home looking for the nameplate with the name Glasser. Inside he found Zachary praying at his mom's bedside that he had found a job as a policeman. Something he knew nothing about, but it would pay her nursing home bills and keep him near her. Wishing to convince him of his longtime possibility of working the Clayton's farm, Manny invited Zachary to dinner with Ellie and him. Zachary had appreciated the job offer, but he was bitter and after dinner he turned it down. Manny's offer was too late. The wounds of losing the farm and how it tore his family apart were too fresh for the young man to do what his heart desired.

Other than for news, which benefited his farm, Manny resisted melting into this rural community, especially since Ellie preferred living in Chicago. Manny was content with their plans to stay the required four years farming and then leave Chester.

Clinging to his well-thought-out plan, he never bothered charming up to the town folks other than Sonny. His grandfather's notes had instructed him to get his basic farm overview from Sonny. Manny's almanac and the books he had purchased on farming could not substitute for the experience or wisdom of Sonny Vinson. His help had been invaluable. But he really did not know him.

Reflecting upon his arrival, the first order from his grandfather's notes was to see Sonny. He recalled Ellie had a headache the day they had planned to join the Vinsons together and review the general planting schedule for the area. Manny wondered if she had intentionally avoided being there with him. His thoughts were running wild. Sitting in the dark with the TV running, he did not like the feeling in the bottom of his stomach. Manny was sure that he was losing Ellie.

Minutes later, he heard the Volvo slip into the driveway. He pulled open the front window blinds to check. It was Ellie. Manny switched on the lights and went to the door to greet her.

"Hey, I was worried about you. Are you OK?" He asked. Holding the door, he rested his weight on one leg while waiting for her response.

"Hey, I'm fine," Ellie remarked, as she moved into the living room where the TV was playing.

"It's kind of late, Babe. Are You sure?" he asked.

"Yes," Ellie said sure that he was suspicious of her late hour return.

Her warm-up was wrinkled and dirty. Carrying her library books in her arms, she hid behind reading glasses. Ellie was spent with all she had held in for too many years. She could only reach for his face and kissed his lips a warm hello, hoping it reassured him. He held her firmly, combating his earlier thoughts. She hugged him until he let go. Manny knew it was not the time to bring up the gossip he had heard about Ellie. In spite of her warm assurance, he was concerned. Manny decided that this Sunday he would follow her. In hindsight he had heard enough sniggering behind his back, and he would see for himself.

CHAPTER SIX

*T*he next morning, Kent was restless and slightly uneasy with his decision to marry Minnie Jean, Chester's newest black schoolteacher. Friday night at Moccasin Pond had been a tumultuous reawakening for Kent that catapulted him into facing another stage of manhood—starting his own family. He had put off marrying in hopes of someday being with Ellie. The night she left him, he had begged the highest heavens to bring her back, a habit he continued under the wide-open sky high above the vast farmland. It provided an open picture for him to dream of their life together like he had for too long. Awakening this morning after the bitter experience of his father with the Sprewells, Kent's dreams were much clearer about what he must do.

Last night for the first time, he decided to stop living in the past, and face the future. Ellie was back, but she was not his. He knew that anymore waiting could now cost them the land. He had let Ellie go physically. But he had to release her emotionally and marry. Could he seal the destiny of being apart from Ellie and go with his plan?

Kent met Minnie Jean when she daringly moved to the small town to teach. After seven years, Chester finally recruited a black teacher willing to bypass the offers from larger school systems or more money. Usually, the college-trained professionals stayed away after receiving their degrees, rarely seeing golden handcuffs in Chester. Folks were proud to know that she walked the school's halls. They were overly excited about the chance of her teaching their children seventh grade math.

Minnie Jean was pretty and single. She wore her hair in a fat French braid with small curls that fell freely about her temple and neck. Thick thighs and long legs sashayed from a size six figure with perfect breasts, waist and hips. She had coffee-colored skin and a nice flat nose. Most of the hard legs sniffed around her like hound dogs on a hunt. It was obvious that Minnie Jean picked Kent as her possible suitor, but he had kept his nose in the farm dirt, acting like he was only half interested.

After three years at the middle school, she asked him to the school's annual Christmas party. He gladly accompanied her wearing a new dark blue suit, a white starched dry cleaned shirt, black dressy boots, and a touch of his dad's "smell good." He took her a small ceramic black angel wrapped in the traditional Rich's Department Store box tied with an oversized gold bow and flowers. Before leaving for the party, she snipped a rosebud and pinned it to her top. They had a good time dancing the shag and doing the electric slide, which was her favorite.

The couple held hands most of the night while talking with the other guest. The two had dated sporadically throughout the year.

The next year, she invited him again to the Christmas party. But the day before, Sonny came down with a touch of pneumonia, and Kent had cancelled to be by his side. It seemed they lost touch after that, except for an occasional church program or town festival. Both were gentle and always kind to the other without making a move to foster a stronger relationship. Since Ellie's return, they had run into each other recently downtown while paying electric bills. Kent showed lesser interest.

This Saturday morning after eating some cereal, Kent grabbed the cordless telephone off the kitchen counter and dialed Minnie Jean. It rang three times as his nerves staggered.

"Hello, it's Minnie Jean." He was about to hang up when he heard her sweet angelic voice.

"May I visit you on Sunday after church?" Kent asked and followed his plan.

"Sure," she agreed, although she was surprised by his call.

She had heard about his prior engagement to Ellie, the new woman in town. The many versions of sordid sad details found their way to her like water flowing downstream. His broken heart and Ellie's disappearance decades ago were out the box and on every tongue. No one ever mentioned what had happened to her until she returned a year ago from Chicago.

Minnie Jean had been admittedly curious about how Kent was taking his first love's return as another man's wife. Her sorrow for him was deep. All curious minds had the same questions. Did he still love her? And were they carrying on where they left off?

The rumblings around town were slanderous and salty. Now that he was calling her, she hoped a relationship with him would slay some of the dragons spurring the gossip in the last year.

✻✻✻

On Sunday, Sonny watched Kent hurry out of the house with an extra spring in his steps, hiding his plan to see Minnie Jean. Sonny racked his brain for what might be happening, a summer festival, a visiting speaker at church or a political rally. Coming up with nothing, he decided to mind his own business.

Kent's face was shaved smoothly. He wore a colorful fancy tie with his favorite gray suit. Before heading out the door, he took his fedora from the mantel where he typically kept it. Loud gospel music played in the background as Kent moved to the door, forgetting his manners to offer his dad a ride.

"See you later," Kent said, walking out of the door.

When he passed him, Sonny caught a sniff of one of his prized colognes, which hid in his chest of drawers. He snickered to himself that Kent had managed to snitch a bottle from his varied collection he had received through the years as Christmas and birthday gifts.

The Vinson men rarely wore the fragrant products except for special times, sticking to their habit of usually preferring just an undetected scent of bland soap. Sonny surmised it was a woman. That was the last time he had dabbed a bit under his chin, when a widowed Eastern Star sister put on a scholarship fundraiser at the church, and Sonny was the deacon in charge.

Kent had prepared Sunday's dinner in the early morning hours before church. When Sonny left, liver and onions still fumed the house. After service, Sonny expected he would eat alone while Kent courted. The two shared most of their dinners every day, so sparing Kent's presence today to see Minnie Jean was fine with Sonny.

Kent hurried to Minnie Jean's house before church was over, forgetting about his usual meeting with Ellie. He eased out of the side door, after counting the collection with the three finance committee members. Ellie noticed when Kent did not come back with the others through the side door, and she watched his spot through the benediction. Gloom set in her face knowing she would miss him after service during fellowship.

Kent drove eagerly the 35-mph speed limit across town, pass the middle school, the supermarket and public swimming pool to Minnie Jean's house on Elks Street. The fourth house on the left with a red door and ivy window box was his destination.

Anxious and way too early, Kent circled the block and headed to the supermarket to kill a little time and to settle down. Kent entered the store and began marching the aisle scanning for something to surprise his date. In the nearly empty store, he went through the express-checkout lane with a couple of items and a Sunday newspaper.

He drove back to Minnie Jean's house, and parked his truck on the street. He pushed the newspaper aside and checked his face in the rearview mirror. He cleared his throat and adjusted his tie, pulling at the knot. Ready to continue his plan, Kent walked along the paved driveway behind her car and up the brick steps. He appeared at her door with a fresh bouquet of mixed flowers and store-bought chocolate chip cookies.

On the steps before ranging the doorbell, he placed the goodies in one hand behind his back. The bell thundered a monstrous sound clear to the outside. While standing on a mat with "Welcome," printed in large letters, the door was opened. Minnie Jean stood, giddy as a schoolgirl, wearing a lime green sundress.

"Hey, I'm so happy to see you," he said smiling. He was no longer nervous and beamed. His free hand touched hers pulling them to opposite cheeks for small kisses.

"Come in, it has been such a long time. Let's catch up." Minnie Jean swept Kent in the door. Seeing the surprises, she said, "Look at you, so kind."

"My pleasure," Kent said, glad that he had.

"I have lemonade set up on the back screened-in porch. Would you like some?" she asked, walking him to the bungalow's backdoor.

"I surely do. If I remember, the porch is really nice and shady," Kent said as he handed her the sweets and a bunch of red tulips with huge orange and pink Gerber daisies gathered in a coat of babybreath's greenery.

"Thank you. How sweet and thoughtful of you to bring flowers and my favorite cookies," she remarked with a big smile, shaking the bag.

Moving the distance to the back of the house, they walked side by side into her living room decorated neatly with French-style furniture in soft matte beige designs. The open floor plan dumped them into the dining room where the table was fully set with plates, glasses, and napkin rings hugging the cutlery. Burgundy was her color scheme. She had soft music playing, filling the rooms with Cab Calloway's Big Band.

"How have you been doing?" Kent asked.

"Fine, it was good to hear from you."

"Let me help you."

"Oh, I've got it, but follow me." She held on to her surprises.

They walked into the kitchen where a two-seat table was centered on a flowery Dhurry rug. All of her small appliances were tucked away, and her countertop clear. She searched momentarily for a vase, opening the doors of two lower cabinets before pulling out a narrow lead crystal one with etched diamond-shape designs around its center. While she was looking, she put aside a platter and dollies. Her bright yellow walls made the small five-by-seven foot area seem cheery and larger. Minnie Jean quickly rinsed and cut the stems under running cold water and placed them in the vase in the center of her tabletop.

Holding her nose to a Gerber daisy and sniffing she said, "These are really special. I love them. Come on."

She beckoned him to the porch where a tall pitcher of lemonade sat in the middle on a round silver tray. Kent sat down on the cozy love seat cushion next to her. He held a glass as she poured. She opened the bag of cookies and spread them making a circle over three dollies on the glass platter.

Turning to look at him with her drink in hand, she offered, "Cheers to a beautiful day."

He tapped his to hers saying, "I'll second that."

They talked for hours about their dreams and hopes for the future. It was like old friends picking up where they left off, never feeling like strangers. Kent sensed a familiar spirit in Minnie Jean. With time he could fall in love with her.

"Do you think you'll stay in Chester?" he asked.

"Well, if the right things fall into place, I might," she told him.

"We're the same age, right."

"Wait, wait a minute, I'm not your age. You've got to be at least four years older, more like five," she said, snickering under her breath.

"Do you want children?"

"Definitely, I like them," she quickly responded, wondering why this question and looking to change the subject, since her doctors recently had ruled out as a possibility her ever having kids.

She smiled during the quiet moments, as Kent appeared to be thinking and offered him more lemonade. Minnie Jean poured a second glass full for him, allowing a sliced lemon ring to settle on his ice cubes.

"Would you like to see my garden?" she asked, changing the subject.

"Yea, let's see what kind of farmer you are. Now, I can be the teacher."

He took a swallow, before standing and letting her pass in front of him to lead the way. Her garden began with short rows of yellow crooked neck squash, cucumbers, and jumbo red tomatoes. The results of her perfect touch greeted him.

"TA DA!" she shouted with her arms spread wide, taking a bow.

"Squash huh, the right color—yellow," he tried hard not to laugh, inspecting the small crop.

He fingered the cucumber vines finding perfect size pickling vegetables. He looked at her smiling.

"They're the right color—green."

Laughing, they both said together, "Tomatoes, the right color—red." Her ready-to-pick vegetables were stilted properly with strings.

"You bet," she basked in his approval.

"I'm afraid you get an 'A' without a doubt." Kent applauded her skills.

Walking arm in arm, they continued their stroll in the backyard, discussing planting. The grass was impeccable, neatly edged with fresh straw. A decorative birdhouse was hanging in a plum tree, which provided a shade where they stopped walking and stood face to face, talking.

"This is a nice place." Kent touched her nose.

"I like it a lot." She rubbed his arm. "Are you ready for some chocolate?"

"How about going to dinner?" he asked as they turned around and headed back to the porch.

"Well, sure, I'd love to."

They went to the cafe and sat in a corner, but the crowd stared. When they entered at six o'clock into a full room, the gossip began. No dragons were slain, just more fire was light in the fine tradition of their small town.

Kent held her hand as they paraded out of the public place with many eyes following them.

After returning to her home, she lit a candle on the enclosed porch. They sat in the swing joking while eating the cookies for dessert. Hours had seeped by before Kent noticed it was getting late.

"Where did the time go?" he announced. Standing up, he stretched while admiring her beauty, saying, "Look at the hour. It's ten o'clock."

"It's been a lot of fun," she said.

Standing, he pulled Minnie Jean close and held her. With their warm bodies snuggled together, his world shifted at that moment. He did not doubt that Minnie Jean would have him and he wanted to marry her. With their faces pressed together cheek to cheek, she felt tears rolling down his face onto hers. Her heart exploded with passion.

With tears of happiness, Kent sat down guiding her to his side. He got on one knee, looking into her eyes. The ceiling fan whipped the crisp evening air, making the candlelight flicker softly. The lemonade pitcher was empty except for lemon seeds at the watery bottom. The leftover cookies were scattered crumbs. The greatest hits of Nat King Cole crooned softly, competing with the night sounds of crickets and bugs that stuck to the screen.

Unable to follow his plan, Kent leaned his head onto Minnie Jean's lap as she wiped his tears with her hand, holding his face as if a delicate flower. Her eyes brightened as their arms wrapped each other, letting the moment take them to pleasant fullness absent for a long time.

EXPECT SUNSHINE

✳✳✳

After Sunday dinner, Manny grabbed his army print shirt and scouted Ellie's path. He stayed out of sight as she led him to the barn on the north border of their property that he thought was all thick woods. He did not know what to expect, sneaking behind his wife.

The farther he traveled in the trees, the harder it was to see. For a few minutes the sunshine disappeared and it turned to ghostly darkness. Manny worried what was under and around his feet. Some of the pathway were covered with moss for a lack of sunlight under the tall trees. But Ellie's weekly trips had made a clear trail worn by her tiny feet.

Manny was close to deciding to give up his chase when he could see light at the end of the thicket. Expecting sunshine, he reached the huge field of tall brown wild grass, amazed at the hidden area. He crouched low seeing Ellie had picked up her pace. She was running to a shelter, which sat near a dozen massive but stunted oak trees. He waited to see if she would enter it.

Ellie appeared child-like skipping along the grassy trail. He had never seen his wife so youthful. Wondering what he would discover, Manny was jealous, some other man caused her to be so excited. She was the serious type who worried too much, and he often reminded her to be calm. But here in a place that he did not know existed, she was different.

Moving closer to Ellie's secret hiding place, he hurried to catch up to her just in case she went past the old barn. He slid behind the closest oak tree, which hid him completely. His pants were dirty from the moments he had crawled along the path staying out of sight. The barn was no longer Ellie's and Kent's or undiscoverable.

It was 4:15 in the afternoon when Ellie reached the barn. She checked her watch thinking Kent would be there soon. She was not so late. As she waited, five o'clock came and no Kent. Ellie paced in odd steps kicking and pointing her toes to busy herself. Feeling like she was wasting valuable time with him being late, Ellie wanted to read to keep her tension down. She decided next time that she would bring a book as waiting made her nervous and brought to her thoughts how wrong this was for Manny.

Six o'clock ticked away and she was still waiting for Kent. But she continued to sit, anticipating and desiring their time together that she longed for each week. Manny watched and wondered. He leaned against the tree knowing something was definitely awry with Ellie. Observing Ellie in the barn, he determined that her weekly trip was not just for time to collect herself. It was too well hidden.

It was getting late, so Manny decided to strike out for home. He studied where he was and saw a path that led in another direction, which cut into the woods further down the open field. To hide his presence, he would not disturb the tattletale grass by making a different path through the picture-perfect brush. Manny wanted to know what Ellie came to the old barn to do and with whom. Wondering, he decided to wait until next Sunday.

Minutes later, Ellie gave up seeing Kent and headed home as whipperpools hollered, signaling it was late.

Exiting the barn, she saw fresh footprints, and was satisfied she had missed Kent.

Manny slammed the back door as he entered the kitchen hungry and angry with Ellie. He changed his clothes before plopping a fat piece of leftover turkey on a plate with collard greens and sweet potato yams. When he sat at the table it was after seven o'clock and Ellie was not home. Whatever it was, Manny knew she took it seriously. To combat his nerves, he picked up the telephone and called his dad.

"Hey, Pops, how's Chicago?"

"Hot as Hades, you heard about the heat wave on the national news?" a voice of a person Manny missed spoke on the other end.

"How's my farmer boy doing these days?"

"Making it Dad, I'm making it." Manny repeated, trying to convince himself things would work out with him and Ellie.

"How's your lovely wife? We miss you both."

Manny heard footsteps hurrying up the back steps, and Ellie entered the house at 7:45 p.m., much later than usual for her Sunday walk.

"Oh, Dad, she's here now. You want to speak to her?"

He handed the phone to Ellie as she entered the house. Without a word, Manny left the table and his plate of untouched food.

***

One week later while preparing Sunday dinner, Ellie burned the fried chicken cooking it in too little grease, too fast. She was rushing to make her meeting with Kent. Last week, she had missed him in the barn, assuming he had showed up early. After what the librarian said and missing him today at church, she now doubted that he had showed.

Ellie reflected on the service, how she had paid little attention to the minister's sermon, looking at every latecomer who had entered the center aisle, hoping for a glimpse of him. She had failed to hear the message, being too concerned with listening to shoes tapping the hardwood floors and wondering if it was Kent. She was ashamed for turning around each time the door opened at the back of the church and staring at the center aisle, studying the who's who of parishioners each time she heard footsteps.

Now, Ellie was annoyed that last Sunday she had also stirred about the barn for hours waiting for Kent and not a word since from him. Standing over her frying pan, an air bubble popped splattering oil and barely missed her arm. She ducked to save her face. She needed to slow down. After putting the heat on medium, she covered the skillet and picked up a book to clear her mind.

Manny sat at the kitchen table peeling red potatoes for his prized potato salad that he liked to eat warm with plenty of finely chopped green onions. He watched her moving fast and debated whether to say what was on his mind. A burnt smell permeated the kitchen escaping the stove fan, which made a harsh noise. Ellie finished cooking and put dinner on the table. She cleared to the side her book with its pages marked near the beginning.

Manny wolfed down his dinner subconsciously pushing Ellie out of the door to follow her again. He had to know as his inside churned with the wrath of what Ellie was doing.

"What are you reading, Dear?" Manny asked, seeing her chunky bookmarker.

The worn and undecipherable bookcover missed its library numbers in coded white writing and its gold foiled stamping on the spine.

"The Grapes of Wrath," she spoke tenderly, now calm after fighting with the fried chicken earlier.

"I liked it a lot when I read it."

"I did, too. It seemed appropriate, so I checked it out this week to read it again." Ellie turned her head and looked at the stove's clock.

Putting her fork down, she offered Manny seconds, hoping he would say no so she could hurry to the barn. Then she would see if the librarian had given her a false bit of news yesterday that Kent was seeing a schoolteacher. She wanted to disbelieve what she had heard about him.

***

Yesterday at the public library, Ellie had dismissed the little old woman who wore her eye specs hanging on the tip of her skinny nose. When she stamped the due date, the librarian had looked up and said, "You her," as if Ellie was to automatically know whom she meant.

But she did know—the same her that left twenty years ago in a wedding dress, reappeared married to the newest farmer in town, and living right next door to the man she stood up. She knew then that people in Chester would never forget.

"Well, you know he's seeing that little teacher down there at the middle school," she said, handing Ellie her book.

She shook as she spoke each word. Ellie was weak in the knees and upset that she had heard such devastating news from a nosey, ninety-year-old looking woman.

Doing an aboutface, she took her borrowed book and had marched away from the gossip. In her Volvo, Ellie drove fast out of the parking lot, squealing the tires. The book slung across the front seat and landed on the floor. She could feel it was true, crushing her heart like something heavy had sat on it.

The divider lines crossed on the two-lane road as she burned with disappointment, feeling the news about the schoolteacher was the reason why Kent had missed their meeting in the barn.

A careless woman who wanted to have her way pointed her car in the direction of home, intending to confront Kent, immediately. Her lips quivered thinking about the rumor. She was ruffled, wondering how could she ever make amends with him, if he paid her no mind.

Driving home, Ellie determined the baby that only she knew about should get his attention. Ellie still remembered how the nurse had whisked the tiny bundle away once she signed the papers, giving her the name Armanda. At Cousin Mae's suggestion, she had made the name request a term in the final documents. It required the adopting family to keep Armanda as her baby's name.

The tiny hands and feet plastered Ellie's thoughts. For two hours, she had kissed the wee toes and cradled the newborn like a doll.

"Two hours," Ellie screamed, nearly running off the road until a semi truck blew its horn, alerting her to a curve ahead.

She had made a hasty decision to give up the baby. Ellie's rashness had gotten her into one misfortune after another. First, running from Mr. Spooky thinking he was dead had changed the course of her life. And giving up the baby did the same. She rationalized that Kent would not consider another woman, if he knew. In the same breath, she knew he could hate her for denying him a choice about the baby. Ellie had pulled off the road in her own front yard with tears streaming from her eyes.

She would think this time and cover her tracks, before deciding what to do about Kent and the schoolteacher. All day and night Ellie had imagined what would bring Kent back. Then she decided.

***

Finished with his Sunday dinner, Manny pushed his chair from the table refusing any seconds.

"No thanks, I'm full," he said and walked away ready for answers. "I think I'll read on the porch. You want to join me?" Manny said, knowing the answer Ellie would give and where she would soon head.

"No, I'm off for my walk. See you later." Ellie cleared the table quickly and left.

Manny waited for her to get a headstart and stretched his arms into the same camouflage shirt that he wore last week, hanging in the mudroom with his field gear. He kept on his black jeans and began his trek for the second time to Ellie's secret place.

CHAPTER SEVEN

*K*ent missed Sunday school and church after staying up late visiting Minnie Jean the night before. Wanting to pop the question, he could not. Something had held him back. Kent started three times to ask her, but each time it was as if he was in a chess game that randomly moved his pieces, when he was ready to propose, and checkmated him to a totally different place than he desired. Kent rolled over in bed when he heard Sonny raising the motor to the truck turning out of the curve pass the mailbox.

Sonny was leaving earlier than usual for a deacon's praise session while Kent slumbered like a baby. The sheets covered him from head to toe and kept it dark for a little extra snoozing. Barely awake, he decided to meet Ellie in the barn to tell her about Minnie Jean and to apologize for not showing up last Sunday. He would tell her before any others took the privilege upon themselves to do so in the fine tradition of gossip in Chester.

It had tickled Sonny to hear the news about Kent and Minnie Jean making its way around town. Sonny could hardly contain his excitement that Kent was serious about a woman. It was just what he needed to protect their land. Sonny had prayed daily that Kent was the key to keeping the farm, hoping that Kent would soon provide an heir. Sonny's prayers were closer to being answered if Kent married her. If Kent was not, Sonny had a Plan B to hold to his promise, which Kent had shrugged off. But Sonny intended to follow it through.

In church, Sonny saw Ellie and Manny in the congregation sitting on the fourth row of pews at the back of the sanctuary. Her head was turned and eyes were glued to the center aisle. Seeing her in a fog, Sonny pondered how she took the news. Surely, she had heard by now.

Finally, Kent got up. He showered and shaved smooth his prickly five o'clock shadow. He put on a pair of jeans with a Michael Jordan tee shirt and headed for the kitchen, contemplating what to cook for dinner. He vacillated between an easy menu of baked sweet potatoes and meat loaf, or taking the time to prepare fresh black-eyed-peas, a baked ham, and sautéed squash. Preferring to rest, he decided on the first choice, which the stove would bake. Stepping barefoot into the kitchen, he felt a bit guilty about missing church.

He tuned the radio to gospel music, and in the large kitchen, he began to rattle pots and pans to the loud rapping hip beat of Kirk Franklin. While praising to the music, he dialed Minnie Jean on the telephone. He talked to her as he washed the potatoes and seasoned the meatloaf, giggling a lot.

"Come over to eat and get to know my Dad," Kent said in haste to make sure he saw her today as he patted the meatloaf into a round shape.

"What are you making?" she asked.

Kent gave to her his full menu along with his shrewd strategy of letting the stove do the work.

"Sounds delicious, hey?" he remarked, "These are old family secret recipes." Kent boasted, wanting to impress her with his cooking skills.

"Right," she echoed back, accepting his impromptu invitation. "What time?" she asked, looking forward to spending time with Sonny.

"Come right now," Kent said smiling. "I can't wait to see you." He was happy.

***

At 3 p.m. sharp after eating a hefty meal with Manny, Ellie anxiously reached the barn, expecting to see Kent. She pressed her fingers on her watch to check the time, unconsciously twisting the side knob and rewinding it. Kent was late, again. Waiting, she opened her book to read, but her mind jumped to what the librarian had said. She would assume it was true, if he did not show today.

Feeling sorry for herself, she made noises to interrupt her thoughts that Kent would not show. Last night, after accepting the possibility of the truth of the words spoken by the nosey librarian, Ellie wrote a letter with all the details of her departure from Chester. She spilled everything to Kent, asking for his forgiveness. Ellie recalled her dreadful bloody fight with Mr. Spooky, and how she assumed he was dead. In a neat hand print, she wrote of how she had refused to help him because he had treated her mother Claudine with contempt all the years they lived with him. Midway, she confessed her lie to Kent about not wanting to be his wife to run away so she could avoid a charge of murder. Lastly, she wrote that she unknowingly carried his baby at the time and put their child up for adoption after a two-hour decision. Ellie's secrets were all explained on paper.

She placed the letter in one of her heavy stock envelopes with flakes of dried lavender she used in love letters while courting Manny. This was Ellie's last resort to stop Kent from leaving her behind, even though there was a risk of her plan backfiring. If she did not tell Kent the truth, the chances were even greater that she would definitely lose his attention to another woman and never win his forgiveness. Ellie had left it unsealed still unsure if she was doing the right thing.

She planned to reconsider the emotional outpour written of her life if Kent showed for their Sunday meeting in the barn like he always had until last week. If he did not show up, she would read it again before making a decision.

She would know soon whether he had intentionally missed her last time. If so with the note, he could not circumvent her plans to communicate with him. Whether he came too early or too late, the next time Kent came to the barn he would get her note. Once Kent read it, he had to see her again, and she hoped it would be to forgive her. The note was an all-or-nothing shot at correcting the mistake she had made twenty-two years ago.

She had anticipated the worst and to protect her place with Kent, Ellie had to tell the truth about the baby and be honest about of her leaving Chester. She had stuck it in her book. Near tears, alone and lonely in the barn, Ellie cracked the novel open and took out what Manny thought was a bookmark. She began to cry.

Not far behind her, Manny had followed Ellie to the abandoned barn, pondering out loud the mess he had made of their lives, bringing them here.

He repeated a mantra as he moved along the path, "I love you Ellie. I love you Ellie."

Manny would not believe the worst. He focused on their union and vows, hoping it was strong enough to keep them together.

He stood near an oak tree farther away from the barn than he had last time. He heard Ellie crying. Part of him wanted to console her, but he watched. Having witnessed Ellie last week impatiently waiting for someone, his mind raced. Today was long with anticipation of what he would see. Since last week, Manny had studied hard why Ellie went to the barn and for what reason.

The sun was setting with Ellie still in the barn, and she wanted to reach out and grab onto it, giving Kent time to finally show. The treetops glowed under a heavy wide ring of dark blue sky like a kid had taken a coloring crayon and outlined them. Manny moved closer and peeked in the window, seeing Ellie curled into a ball, weeping softly.

Suddenly, she stopped and he instantly ducked. She unfolded the note and began to read. Once she finished, her sadness mellowed.

Down low and out of sight, he heard her rustling on the hay. Carefully looking inside, Manny watched Ellie seal it with her red lips and place the white square envelope partially between two bales of hay at eye level and leave.

When she reached the trees disappearing from sight, Manny left his hiding place and walked into the barn. He went to the letter and took it. Holding what could have answers for him, he easily opened it without tearing the folded flap. It was freshly sealed but still damp. He read it mesmerized. His inside hurt, and he felt lightheaded. Now, he fully understood whom Ellie came to see in the barn and for what reason. He had answers. They were not easy to take or comfortable.

Reviewing Ellie's reaction to moving to Chester, he now understood why she had protested coming back. Although he had pushed her, Manny felt sorry for asking Ellie to leave Chicago. The letter read of someone in great pain. Moving to Chester, he had caused his wife a lot of grief.

In the note, Manny learned that the man she was meeting had been Kent, her fiancé more than twenty years ago. Even greater, that she had been pregnant with Kent's child and did not know it on the night she fled Chester, thinking she had killed Mr. Spooky, his grandfather. Grasping the full tenor of her statements and from her description in the letter, he concluded that his grandfather must have been a mate to her mother Claudine. His knees grew weak.

Manny knew that Ellie was hiding something about Chester, but he never suspected all this. She was a mother to a grown daughter a child put up for adoption in Chicago. That meant he had a stepdaughter. He could not believe what the sweet-smelling paper said to him or the bits of lavender flakes. He was crushed by her actions and kicked in the hay. Manny was not sure what to do with the letter, so he resealed it with the wet lips. Then he reached up to replace it, but he stopped and began his journey home.

Ellie entered her front yard looking to see Manny sitting in his favorite rocking chair where she had left him enjoying the newspaper. Her landscaping efforts had paid off as the gladiolus and snapdragons bloomed fully and as heavenly as clouds. Lots of ground covering with purple tips circled their L-shaped flowerbeds on both sides of the porch. In a day or two, Ellie was planning to paint the steps white to match the door and plant an array of colors along the hedges. A wind chime hanging on the banister made a low jangle, sending a lovely sound to her ear. She appreciated the sweetness amid all the sadness of her day. The stray cat slithered around her ankles as Ellie stood in the yard, wondering where to start to refresh the annuals and her life.

She would give Kent had one more week to show up, or she would visit him. He was her best friend and she missed him terribly. Had she done the right thing by telling him everything on paper, rather than face to face?

"Ellie, Ellie," came from a voice of someone walking alongside of the house.

117

Thinking it was Kent, she took off skipping steps from the porch and rounded the corner of the house, running straight into Manny's arms. They bumped hard into each other.

"Wow," he yelled, catching Ellie and looking into her eyes.

She glanced down unable to withstand the guiltiness she felt about Kent.

He lifted her chin to bring them eye to eye and said, "Honey, I love you."

Manny hugged her tightly while seeing the letter flash before his eyes.

***

Sonny came home from church dragging his double-breasted coat as he entered the house and yelled, "Kent, I'm home." He had seen the burgundy Maxima in the yard and parked near it in the wide space before the grass.

Kent yelled from the kitchen, which opened up under a large arch to the main sitting room where Sonny entered, "Come here, I want you to say hello to somebody." He pulled at Sonny's hand bringing him closer to their dinner guest. "This is Minnie Jean, you remember her pictures I showed you in the newspaper. Isn't she pretty?" he spoke, admiring his lovely girlfriend.

"How do you do? And my goodness she's more than pretty, Son." Sonny reached to hug her.

"I'm so happy to see you," she said, while pressed into his warm embrace. Finding her chair opposite of Kent with one for Sonny at the head of the table, she smiled at the charming older gentleman.

"I hope you're hungry. Dinner is ready."

"Let me wash up. We had three people to join for baptism, a whole family," Sonny said. "It took a while to extend the right hand of fellowship to the entire congregation." Looking at Kent, he joked, "I'm giving that deacon spot to you, Son, and soon."

Leaving the room, Sonny motioned for Kent to come with him by wiggling his right forefinger three times.

"Excuse us Minnie Jean, I'll be right back." Kent puckered up his lips and blew her a kiss in the air as he migrated to the other room behind his father.

"What's up, Dad?" he asked with a big grin on his face.

"I saw Ellie running along the northside border on her husband's property a few minutes ago. You think she's alright?" Sonny asked, concerned that Ellie might be reacting to hearing the latest on Kent.

"Sure, she's probably fine," he said as he hunched his shoulders implying that he really did not know.

What he did know was that she was headed to the barn to meet him. "Darn it!" Kent spoke under his breath, realizing that he had forgotten all about Ellie in spite of his intentions this morning to meet her.

Sonny went into the bathroom and closed the door. He immediately turned the faucet on and water spewed out. Kent suppressed the thought of his missing the weekly meeting with Ellie, hearing the water stream. Ellie would be disappointed, again. Last week he was on a mission that had precluded him from seeing her, and this week he honestly forgot. Kent was stupefied, but what could he do now that the woman he would ask to marry him stood at the dinner table, waiting.

Back in sight of his date, Kent said, "Have a seat, I'll finish setting the table." He motioned for Minnie Jean to take a seat as he pulled her chair out. "Are you ready for the best meal you've had in weeks?" he stated, perking up while he fixed their serving tray.

"Yea, and with the most handsome man I know," she sassily quipped.

"It sure smells good in here." Sonny came to the table, rolling up his sleeves.

"Oops, let me make that the two most handsome men I know," Minnie Jean quickly corrected herself.

They laughed, as Kent was burdened with how to handle Ellie, after missing her in the barn two weeks in a row.

CHAPTER EIGHT

*E*arly Monday morning, the telephone rang buzzing a solid sound followed by three short dings, which broke the silence in the Clayton's house. Ellie thrashed about in a bubble bath in one of the master bathrooms.

Hearing it ring four times, she yelled sending her cry through the large fully tiled space. "I'm in the tub!"

"I'll get it." Manny shouted, wrestling with making up the bed.

He answered to the voice of Sonny asking, "Can you come over? We need to talk."

"Today?" Manny regarded.

"Yes, if you can," Sonny's aging tone managed in a serious way.

"Absolutely, sir," Manny respectfully stated, "How about around eleven this morning?"

"Good timing, I'll have Kent come home early for lunch and join us," Sonny agreed.

"See you then," Manny said, wondering what in the world Sonny wanted and did it have anything to do with Ellie.

"Thanks, young man, good-bye," Sonny said and hung up.

"Who was it?" Ellie asked as she dried off with a bright orange towel.

Stepping onto a fuzzy mat next to the garden tub, Ellie melted her feet into pink slippers with feathers around the mouth. She had heard Manny talking for a while, but she was unable to decipher who or what. Ellie paused to hear his response.

"It was the Vinsons wanting to see me today." Her husband yelled through the huge bedroom across their half made-up, king-size bed.

He stopped what he was doing and walked through a sitting area separating them. He passed between two loveseats facing each other with a heavy walnut wood coffee table in the center. On its polished tabletop, a large picture book on African-American art was sprawled on the left with Manny's favorite wedding picture. He waited at the bathroom's door.

"Oh!" Ellie said alarmed but she hesitated to ask for any details.

"Did you hear me?" he asked, cracking the door to speak through, trying to detect if Ellie gave any clues by her reaction.

"Yes."

Ellie was quiet, so he headed downstairs to go to the field. She took her time placing on her deodorant and lotion as she sat on a boudoir stool.

"Honey, I'll come home early for lunch and leave from here for the Vinsons after cleaning up and changing from my field clothes. Will you lay something out for me to wear?" Manny asked as he went downstairs. His plea carried louder when he raised his voice, making sure it reached Ellie. She took her shirt from a hanger and put it on silently, thinking.

"OK!" Ellie yelled back, hearing him as she moved quietly into the bedroom, partially dressed in a large blue button-down shirt while looking for a pair of jeans to put on.

She had completely missed Manny who was at the bottom of the stairs, gathering his field gear and a raincoat.

"If I'm not here, I'm taking the book back to the library, alright," she yelled when she did not see him.

As she shouted to Manny downstairs, her mind juggled the afterthought of catching Kent before lunch to see what was brewing. When the door shut behind Manny, Ellie took the time to think clearly. She wondered what the visit with Sonny and Kent was all about.

Curious about whether or not Kent had actually gotten the letter, Ellie hurriedly finished dressing, putting on hiking boots and tying a bandana on her hair before going to the barn to see. She smelled the tractor fumes where Manny had pulled off minutes earlier. Dew sparkled on the short cut grass and covered with a mist her dirt flowerbeds. A string of meows from the bushes caused Ellie to pause and look for the cat.

She took it as a sign to be calm. When she left the barn close to eight o'clock last night, it would have been way too dark to navigate the briers and stumps in the heavily wooded trees. Surely, the letter was still stuck between the bales of hay where she had left it.

Ellie hoped Manny's tractor continued south as she pressed on northward off the main road, occasionally checking to see his direction. Dust attacked her boots as she walked the dry dirt trail just off the roadway. Minutes later, she was safe almost out of sight to the trees and relaxed a bit, taking in the birds chirping and the stillness of early morning. Her favorite time of the day was a little cooler than normal. She heard thunder rumblings in the distance.

A horn blew as Ellie trotted. It sounded longer a second time trying to catch her attention, so she turned to face the sound, knowing Manny would be there. And he would ask what she was doing.

Her cheeks blushed under the embarrassment of getting caught. Looking around to face her fate, it was Kent in a dark Chevy. On the road in a swirl of dust moving toward her, his truck puttered to a stop, as the trailing dust encased the vehicle. Disappearing into thin air, it settled over the field. They were yards away from each other and a good distance from her house when a thick cloud in the sky sent a shadow over them.

A ball of nerves, Ellie waved as he pulled off the main road onto the shoulder. Already shaken, she guessed he knew about the child, and it was too late to retrieve the letter. He was coming to see her like she had planned. But she was nervous she had lost him by being cruel and careless with such tender news of him being a father. On a night's rest, she had resolved the note was the wrong thing to do. But it was done.

Kent looked concerned, waving as he walked toward her. Ellie stayed where she was prolonging the outcome of the news she wrote in his letter, which had spurred pain each day of her life for over twenty years. Too long buried in her heart, and now written in the note, her secrets were known. Feeling at Kent's mercy, she looked down to avoid his eyes. She could tell by his approach that he was not about to forgive her, and her world of being in his good graces would soon crack like an egg and ooze the last bit of attachment necessary to hold her life together.

"Ellie," Kent spoke coming closer.

"What?" she spewed in fear, disbelieving the turn of events was unlike what she had planned.

She had worried about Manny catching her, not once thinking Kent would be the culprit standing between her and the note in the barn. Surely, he had it, and her chance of easing into his forgiveness—gone.

"I know I came without calling," he began and adjusted his cap, which advertised a heavy farming equipment company. "We need to talk. It couldn't wait," he added, moving within a few feet of her and holding up his hands crossing them repeatedly as if motioning to deny what he or she would say next.

"Now you know." Ellie cut him off ready to defend her long held secrets. She said in quick biting words, "And I hope you understand." She wanted to curse, but a lump formed in her throat.

"I'm sorry and I apologize." Talking at the same time she was, Kent responded to his failure to give Ellie the news of his intentions to marry Minnie Jean. "But I have to think of having a wife and a family of my own one day. And Minnie Jean is a nice woman." He rambled on clueless.

"What?" Ellie spat out, beginning to realize that Kent was talking about something totally different than she.

"We can't be together, Ellie. You belong to Manny. It's just that simple, and I'm letting go." He put his hand on his hips like Ellie had hers, which rested on the belt loops of her tight fitting jeans. "Our meetings are over," he said, looking into her eyes. Ellie was astounded that he had not gotten the note.

The wind picked up blowing dust, bringing the smelled of rain. The dark cloud grew wider when Ellie turned her back to Kent momentarily, debating with herself whether to tell him what he did not know about their baby. If she told him, would it stall his plans to get involved with another woman? So confused with her options, Ellie's mind flipped from what her mission was this morning of concealing the news in the note to now, offering it on a silver platter to Kent. She was jealous, wanting the news in her note to stop him and the schoolteacher. But would he forgive her like she wanted him to? That was the question she needed answered.

"Turnaround and talk to me, Ellie," Kent demanded.

"Could I say anything to change your mind to marry this woman?" Ellie offered, really afraid that she was losing her chance at forgiveness and her best friend.

"No, Ellie, it's no longer about me. It is bigger than you know."

He told her the whole story of the Moccasin Pond deal and about the promise Sonny had made to his grandfather to hold on to their land. Ellie was flabbergasted learning of the trouble Sonny had faced.

Processing the end result of what would happen under the deal to the Vinson's land, Ellie knew her selfish need to hold on to Kent was not important to him. He needed to provide an heir for the land, and he would not let her stand in his way any longer.

Surely, Kent would hate her for holding the fact that an heir already carried the Vinson's blood, but he just did not know it. It was her fault that he did not know. Was it best to let him move on with his plans? Under the circumstances, she could keep the fact of her adopted child buried in the past, sparing everybody the pain of the naked truth.

"You see, Ellie. It has nothing to do with you, or the way I feel. I won't let my dad down." Kent firmly stated with his mind made up.

"What if?" Ellie rankled as she saw the handwriting on the wall that it was now or never to talk about their child.

Still unsure of what to do, she stuttered talking fast with her hands.

Kent interrupted Ellie saying, "There are no ifs."

Her heart sank. Then he held Ellie's hand and he raised it to his lips. He kissed for the last time the hand of the only woman he ever loved. He held her hand to his face. Holding it there, she trembled as a cloud rolled overhead and burst with a tumultuous boom, showering them with rain. Huge pellets fell. Covering Ellie in his arms from the flying dust and rain, Kent grabbed her and pressed forward out of the sudden downpour to his truck.

"No," Ellie fought to get loose wanting to retrieve the letter that could ruin her.

"Ellie, it's too dangerous to be out." They stopped and she grappled free.

A hurricane blew close somewhere beyond the fields of the South Georgia town near the Florida coast. The wind roared blowing them to stoop low and protect their faces.

"I'm going home from here." Ellie could not take a chance on the letter leaving the barn.

"Get in the truck, Ellie." Kent moved her by the elbow to his passenger door and put her in. "I know you remember these summer hurricanes, and how it can take you or any of these trees down," Kent said as he cranked the vehicle and pulled onto the road to drive Ellie home.

The windshield wipers whisked fast barely clearing his vision to see the road in the bad weather. Kent drove as close as he could to her house and stopped. Clamoring one last time to earn her peace from the man that she felt it was necessary to love, Ellie mumbled and botched her words.

"Go Ellie, it's over." Kent interrupted her.

Out of the truck, she slammed the door, and he drove away, out of her life.

Stepping out the weather and into her house, the violent thunderstorms had kept Ellie from reaching the barn where she had stuck the sealed envelope between two bales of hay. After the storm, Ellie wondered if it would be where she had left it.

Easing the stress of her initial concern that Sonny wanted to discuss the note's contents with Manny, Ellie's heart fluttered. She could not settle her nerves. After seeing Kent, she felt safe that he wanted Manny for something else.

Hearing Kent's news to marry made Ellie lament the ugly possibility and close call of them learning the existence of the child. It was the one secret she believed could cause everyone grief, so she decided no one would ever know. It would forever be her secret.

Her only peace in Chester would be to have a second child and make amends for the wrongs she had done. Inside her home, Ellie sat on the living room sofa, finding her composure and occasionally jumping when loud thunderclaps burst and flashed.

Out of rage, Ellie had come close to losing everyone she cared about, including Manny. At the first let up in the stormy weather conditions, she would go for the letter written out of spite with her secrets in the barn. Then Ellie would bury the note like she would any feelings for Kent.

Kent was no longer hers.

***

Ellie picked khakis and a green golf shirt for Manny to wear to the Vinsons and laid them at the foot of the bed, knowing the weather would cancel the meeting. Not as nervous as she was earlier when she thought the letter was a threat, Ellie was now less concerned about Sonny wanting to talk with Manny and went about her duties. She was so thankful her troubles were over.

The lights flickered and temporarily went out. She searched for a flashlight and candles to have them ready. Ellie pulled back the laced kitchen curtains looking for Manny and saw his tractor sitting in the field. Suddenly, she heard a crash in the front room and ran to see what was the matter. Manny rushed in dripping wet.

"I let everyone go home. It's a storm coming." Manny said, taking the stairs.

He peeled off his wet clothes. Walking the steps beside him, Ellie plucked each piece during their first summer hurricane together in Chester.

In the bedroom, Manny dried off and put on the golf shirt and khakis.

"Thanks for the clothes, I'm not going out, but I really need them, now." He smiled. "I'll call the Vinsons in a few minutes," Manny said, taking the damp clothes from Ellie and putting them away.

He went to his study to make the call. The wind sang and growled as it carried debris pass his window. The sky was blue black. Manny hesitantly dialed the telephone, wondering if it was safe. Sonny answered on the other end of the line.

"Hello, Mr. Vinson, I need a rain check on getting over," he proposed. "Can it wait?"

"Yes, indeed," Sonny agreed, wanting to rush off the telephone in the bad weather.

"Sir, one second, if you will. There is a barn and a huge grassy field I never knew existed from seeing the land survey. Where do you understand the north border to be between our properties?" Manny asked, getting anxious about his plans for Ellie's hideaway.

Sonny gave his version of an imaginary line being vertical from the farthest oak tree from the back of the barn.

"Thank you, I think I'm going to cut some timber there and mow the grassy field soon. May I help you with the same?" Manny offered his plan to rid the barn of its privacy.

Sonny was content with his border and declined his help to clear his portion. Just then the line popped, and the telephones cut off.

CHAPTER NINE

It had been forty-eight hours since the hurricane watch began with heavy rain and flooding. At the crest of sunrise, Sonny had walked some of the farmland surveying for storm damage. He needed a new tin tub for watering the hogs, because one of his prized two hundred-pound plus heifers had knocked one flat, moving inside a crowded covered hog pen during the storm. He saw where an old pecan tree beginning to rot was split in half, but everything else had survived. Sonny was expecting sunshine as he prepared to do his mid-week shopping at the local hardware store and the Weed & Feed Shop.

While there, he would buy fertilizer, a blade file to sharpen his plowing disks, and a box of snub-nose nails to start repairing the back fence he had noticed was weak months ago and surely had succumbed to the weather last night.

Under bright sunshine that shone on what could be a perfect day, Sonny and Kent drove into town on the mucky wet and likely washed out roads. They were going to the Weed and Feed Shop first and then the local hardware store. Their light blue '74 Ford truck, used for hauling on the farm, was in tiptop shape. It plowed the thick grooves in the dirt roads leading into town. Due to the expected road conditions, Sonny had cheated on using his newest Chevy truck, a '96 model, which usually made the Wednesday routine trips of the Vinson men.

Warming up the engine, the two debated on where the most damaged spots on the route would be.

"I think near the steeple church at the V, washed-out for sure," Sonny offered, looking out of the wide cabin.

He sat his "To Buy" list on the black vinyl dashboard, which was peeling in long slashed rolls. Fiddling to get comfortable sitting between the torn springs, they rubbed off dust from the seat onto their jeans and coveralls. With each movement they made, the cotton stuffing scattered and collected on the floorboard among tools and old metal parts.

"Well, you 'bout right. Don't forget the usual slidefest before the wooden bridge near the paved road junction," Kent said, scrubbing the gears. "What a mess that will be." He jerked into first after jumping from neutral, rolling out of park.

"The county probably emptied the jails for sandbagging," Sonny figured.

"Dad, I'm hungry. Are you?" Kent asked, getting used to the feel of the old hardly used truck and rubbing his stomach to show him.

"Yep, your treat. I'll tip." Sonny laughed as they came to the V near the church, traveling on the messy roadway. The road was washed out under a pool of water. "Go easy here, Son," Sonny said, ending the chuckling as he leaned into the dashboard like it would assist traversing through the water. Water was reaching up to the doors and sweeping in under their shoes, it was a hazard.

"More to the right, away from the dip, see how the hood is sitting," Sonny masterfully detected.

"OK, Dad," Kent followed the suggestion of the wiser older farmer who had driven these same roads for over sixty years. "We're making it," Kent said determined to get through the few washed out yards.

Each year, Sonny had lobbied the county for paved roads, but it was slow getting the main arteries fixed. He understood every road, lane, or byway was not created equally, and the county coffers would go broke pleasing everyone. There were too many fields and borders to pave or consider for gravel. The best Sonny could do was bargain for a regularly maintained hard dirt road leading to their property. It was scraped monthly when the bulldozing machine removed rocks, cut the ditches, and leveled a smooth path.

In town, a few large trees were blown down exposing a bundle of roots lifted completely out of the earth. But the hundred-year-old, solid brick and mortar buildings held up relentlessly under the first hurricane of the season.

Kent parked in front of the cafe where lights in the busy spot showed it was packed with people who had been cooped up for a few days, dying to get out.

"Bet you all the money I got, Tall Nancy is waiting for us," Sonny said, maneuvering the steep step-down from the old truck.

"No way man, I play better odds than that." Kent signaled with a thumbs down to the deal.

Inside, they began eating a peaceful breakfast in a booth near the back away from the fray. Covering the table in front of them were fresh sausage patties and biscuits for Kent and oatmeal with ham and three eggs for Sonny, plus coffee for both.

Near them the people were noisy, smoking and complaining about their damage during the storm. A whole fence down, a barn leveled, and a tree landing on a nearly new car were the stories Tall Nancy carried from spot to spot, scuffling in cheap shoes as she traveled the dining area pouring seconds of coffee.

"How yawl?" she asked as she spotted the Vinson farmers half-finished with eating their breakfast. Holding a round glass pot of steaming black coffee, Tall Nancy poured each a sip.

"We're doing fine; a little muddy," Sonny said, lifting his combat boots and sticking them in the aisle.

"We'll have you cleaning this place, so watch out there," she quipped. "It's rather sloppy outside, so you're off the hook this time. The good thing is we're in business today. Yesterday..." she stopped to wiped sweat from her brow with a free hand and put the coffeepot down. Catching her breath, she continued, "Yesterday, this

empty place scared me. You thought it was a ghost town."
She puttered about the table gathering the empties and
placing fresh napkins from her apron pocket out at the
corner of the booth.

"Did you hear?" Tall Nancy began to sing like a record
player.

"Ms. Nancy, somebody over there is calling you,"
Kent said, pointing to the tables pushed against the
opposite wall near the coatrack. Kent was not in the
mood for any gossip, today.

Tall Nancy turned around and saw wiggling fingers
pushed through a raggedy old glove of a snaggled-tooth
Sprewell sitting all alone, beckoning her to come.

"Excuse me, I'll be right back," the tired and
forever-talking waitress shuffled away.

The men ate rapidly the cold oatmeal and the last bite
of sausage with little conversation. Leaning back with a
full stomach, Sonny scoped his wallet for his list and a
tip.

Putting them both on the table, he asked, "You see'd
my list? Do we need to add anything?" Sonny looked at
Kent as he pinched the torn piece of paper.

"Well, we'll see at the Weed & Feed Shop. Are you
ready?" Kent inquired, searching the room to see where
Tall Nancy stalked.

Still across the room, she nodded her head while
talking to an angry Sprewell who was sending a message
to Sonny. Kent waved good-bye to her as he scrubbed
across the rubbery cushion and got out to help Sonny
from his seat. Sonny's boots tracked his path through the

café to the cashier where Kent counted five dollars and handed it to the owner.

They were hurrying into the street when Tall Nancy waved to catch their attention to relay his message. The fellows moved on, mistaking her motion for another good-bye.

"Jump in, Dad," Kent rushed. "Let's get going or this will take all day."

He cranked the old truck, which sallied out of the parking lot with his heavy foot on the pedal.

"Son, I'm glad we got each other." Sonny laughed at Kent's clowning and imitating the old truck choking out the café parking lot.

Kent drove the rusty blue truck crossed the square to the angled parking spaces near the latticed front shop. He nudged the stick shift into park and stopped an equal distance between the two stores. The entrance to the sidewalk was wet and slippery with puddles. The pair shopped for the listed items. As Kent located each one, Sonny followed behind him, striking through the list with a lead pencil. Going from one store to the other, it took them twenty minutes to finish.

Returning home, it was sprinkling rain as they exited the small town's square and descended on the two-lane road where the county prisoners, like Sonny had imagined, worked the slough. A red flag waved the traffic to traverse the safe side as the men in white uniforms with a dark stripe along the pants seams lifted sandbags to fill and balance the washed out road.

Two sheriff's vehicles were anchored on the shoulder of the road, and one Chester police car with its motor

running was parked in front of the workers. The police
red lights blinked as white exhaust escaped billows of
smoke. The driver's side door was left opened wide, and
the assigned officer, Zachary Glasser, stood poker faced,
holding a shotgun on a line of seven men. A farmer's boy
all his life, he was just three months on the force trying to
support his mother after their farm was foreclosed.

"Easy, here Kent," Sonny echoed, having assumed the
inmates would be needed after the storm.

Kent maneuvered the old vehicle and passed a big
hauling truck, which carried whopper-sized sandbags,
poles and wood for repairing bridges. With a minimum
distance of ten car lengths to travel before they could
gather speed and go home, Kent waited for the red flag to
signal him.

Gripping tightly his issued weapon like he was taught
in a six-week police course, Zachary nodded at the
Vinsons. An entourage of four cars was in front of them.
Directing traffic on the better side of the road, the
flagman rested his sign signaling them to proceed. The
bumper to bumper traffic in front of the old pick-up
inched pass one by one. Moving a short distance, Kent
tapped the gas, but the red flag coasted up and he skidded
to a stop and was the sole vehicle waiting.

The men with bold numbers on their chest heaved and
puffed under the weight of the bags. Some sang to the
motion to ease the heavy load, others whistled. But the
rain began to fall heavily, and the team of workers was
order to gather their tools. With the repair not yet
completed, their drudgery had ended. One sheriff's
vehicle drove away in the direction of the city limits.

First, a soft drizzle and now the heavier ran was making the sunny day doom.

"Looks like they did a decent job," Sonny announced, watching the men disband and line up to board the prison bus.

"I can't wait to get home. I thought it wasn't suppose to rain today," Kent said as he picked up speed.

The last prisoner broke the single-file line and ran. A flash of white caught Officer Zachary's eye as the prisoner jumped into the rear of the Vinson's truck. Shots were fired in rapid succession. Heads ducked as the sound ripped the air. One bullet hit the tail of the old truck and the other its rear window shattering the glass, causing Kent to loose control of the vehicle.

"Hey, son!" Sonny belted. "Keep it in the road!"

Seeing him slumping over the steering wheel, Sonny leaned to Kent's side and put his foot on the brakes. He managed a stop before running into the flooded ditch. Kent's head drooped, and he grasped his neck. He was hit.

More shots rang out like target practice.

"Son, you're hit! Somebody help!" He shouted as Zachary raced to the driver's side window, banging and screaming that he was sorry.

In a state of distress, the shooter flung opened the door crying. "The medics are on the way. It's radioed into headquarters. I'm so sorry, please forgive me." He pleaded as he helped Kent out of the truck.

Holding onto his son, Sonny crawled from the same side, asking for mercy.

"Don't die on me, Kent!" Sonny hollered as he held his only son who gasped for each breath.

With his eyes steady on his Dad's, Kent mumbled, "Ellie. Ellie. Now, I know why she was never mine." Trying to speak, he muffled, "I would have left her all alone." He was weak with great peace in his eyes.

"Ssssshh," Sonny said, trying to soothe him. Seeing his eyes closing, he could only hope Kent would not die.

Zachary heard Kent's words about Ellie. The young officer immediately ran to his car and took off, fearing that Kent might die at his hands.

"Dad, I'm going to...." Kent faded out with Sonny clutching him in his arms while holding up his head.

He jerked once with his eyes still closed.

Sonny screamed, "Noooo! This can't happen to me!"

He looked around in anguish as the medics rushed to help Kent, a little too late. They pulled the hurting father aside and began an attempt to resuscitate Kent.

***

At 11:05 a.m., Ellie's stomach flipped sending a wave through her body, jarring her from a deep sleep. She sat up searching the room, feeling like she did not know where she was. Earlier, she woke up still worrying about the note in the barn, but then fell back asleep. During the last two days, she had wallowed in the fear of getting the letter after the storm. With her hair scattered over her head, she realized the wind had subsided and the weather was finally clearing.

She smelled Manny's morning coffee, which communicated to her that he was already out in the fields, catching up on lost days of production on the farm. His bedcovers were on her side making her movement cumbersome. Sweating from the heat produced by the extra cover, she freed her body, pushing the comforter to her feet. Her pajama top was sweaty. Unsure if she had dreamed or had a foreboding omen, Ellie was uncomfortable with the rush that jarred her awake.

"Was it her Cousin Mae in Chicago?" she asked herself.

A little unnerved by her sixth sense, she slid to the bedside and rang her cousin, still in a daze.

"Hello, Cousin Mae, it's Ellie," she said, getting her equilibrium.

"Child, it's been a month of Sundays since I heard from you. Missy, girl how you doing?" Her heavy and manly voice bellowed to Ellie who began to drop tears.

"I'm fine, are you?" Ellie asked, wanting to rule Cousin Mae out and forget the busy butterflies that turned her stomach.

Spending a few minutes catching up on their lives, she felt better before Cousin Mae hurried off the telephone to do her volunteer work. She held the telephone in her hand not knowing whom else to call. She went to her windows and searched for a sight of Manny. First parting the heavy chintz treatment at the north window and then the south's, she saw his tractor pulling a disk plowing in the field. Her heart pounded as she surveyed the view and tried to settle her senses. Was this a sign to get the letter before it was too late?

Without taking a shower, Ellie dressed in old jeans, a long sleeve shirt and rubber boots. Picking up speed to hurry before Manny would come home for lunch, she pulled her springy hair into a scrunchy, washed her face with a splash of running water, and quickly brushed her teeth. Before shutting the backdoor, Ellie grabbed a rain slicker from the mudroom. She raced down the steps and over the black and white cat, causing him to scream and attack her foot.

"Sorry, little one," she said as it braced for a fight, and she jumped over him.

She trotted nervously on the path to the barn, hoping the weather had not diverted her chance to destroy the note. In the wrong hands, this could end her marriage and cause unnecessary grief. She cleared the trees where some limbs were broken and splintered like matchsticks. Trotting faster through the tossed grass, Ellie saw the abandoned barn and knew it had suffered some damage. Several pieces of tin on the rooftop were rolled like cans that twisted back with the little keys. A ripped off layer made the windowless opening wider. Its frame remained strong but its body was weakened by the storm. Tongues of the wind had licked up the straw from inside and spit it outside. Hay was loosened from its fragile bindings and began a path as she entered the barn hit by the storm, but standing.

Near the post, Ellie's eyes fell on the spot where she had placed the note, and it was gone. Frantically, She scrutinized the entire area for a speck of white. Nothing. She moved rapidly the length of the barn, kicking up the scattered hay. Becoming alarmed, she crawled over the remaining stacks and slid to the barn's backside. After rumbling through, Ellie was somber at the inevitable fact that she would not find the note. Scornful that her life's secrets had obviously floated out of her hands, Ellie could only pray that the storm had destroyed it.

Outside of the barn, she traced a wide circumference of the trees except the farthest one away, hoping for a glimpse of the tiny note in the tossed, bitten, chewed off and disturbed grass. She searched in vain. There was not a sign of the letter in or around the barn. Ellie's minutes were up. Manny would be home soon, so a muddy and upset Ellie wandered back in the direction of the brick house to fix her husband's lunch.

She went through the trees and beelined for the main road. After accepting the fact that the letter was lost, she sprinted to make better time when a car was coming behind her. She made wide heavy strides, moving fast, but her galoshes sunk repeatedly in the soft dirt, slowing her down. Hearing the motor roar, Ellie peered over her shoulder and saw a police vehicle pressing toward her, flashing its red lights without the siren.

Ellie stood to the side for it to pass, but she watched it come to an abrupt stop at her feet. Zachary, Maze County's newest officer, jumped out and met her. Fretting, he tried to speak spilling out words, which sounded like nonsense to her.

"Ms. Ellie, it happened so fast, my fault, I'm not cut out for this..." He rattled in broken sentences, throwing Ellie off as she listened to what likely had churned her insides this morning.

"Wait, wait slow down young man," she said with mixed emotions of him attempting to tell her bad news in spite of the gloom she was already feeling.

Ellie touched his arm as he continued to gnaw on his words making incomplete thoughts out of his story. Right in front of her, Zachary, dressed in an official police uniform with a pistol at his waist, was crying through his message.

"OK, just catch your breath," she demanded as Zachary fidgeted looking around while being comforted by her. Unable to speak, he was silent behind facial expressions that showed grief.

"What is it?" Ellie asked, getting the same feeling that had awakened her. Then she screamed, "It's Kent?"

The novice officer nodded his head uncontrollably.

"Where? How? When?" Ellie spat her questions.

Zachary mustered, "Get in."

Ellie did without thinking twice. Once in the car, Zachary turned a "180" on the wet road, gunning the engine to avoid getting stuck. They sped off to town.

"Is he alive?" Ellie asked him as she held onto the door tightly in her seatbelt.

It pressed against her chest due to the many false stops and abrupt slow downs Zachary made while dodging through traffic without sounding the siren, which he had not learned how to use.

Responding through tears, he took a deep breath and said, "I don't know, Ma'am." His voice trembled. Still rushing, he rammed the vehicle up to the hospital's front door, and Ellie leaped out with Zachary on her heels. In the emergency waiting area, Sonny grabbed Ellie as she whipped through the corridor.

"Let me go!" she shouted. "Where is he?"

Zachary sparred with Ellie to help Sonny control her. They wrestled her to the floor where she succumbed, crying.

Sonny knelt down beside Ellie and hugged her, saying repeatedly, "He's gone."

CHAPTER TEN

*M*anny decided to skip lunch and attack the tree cutting and grass mowing on the border like he had mentioned to Sonny. Early this morning, he contacted a pulpwood company to meet him at noon. While plundering around his tractor shed, he heard the large machinery pull into the yard, and he waved them to follow him. He expected Ellie would bring him food, once she realized that he was too busy to return home to eat.

Manny crossed the field with the crew ready to oblige him in getting rid of Ellie's secret place. At the thicket, he gave the foreman his instructions to cut any trees more than eight inches wide and to remove any dead or broken limbs. The majority of the trees would come down, as they stood too tall and larger than eight inches round. He was hoping his act of clearing the border to the abandoned barn would bring Ellie to talk about her secrets.

He had carried her note in his hip pocket each day, since lifting it from the spot where Ellie had placed it. Since last Sunday, Manny had been considering how to discuss the contents with her. But he could not find the right segues for talking about—what he was not supposed to know.

Manny planned to ride over after work today to Sonny's and talk as Sonny had requested before the storm had called off their meeting. Manny was quite uncomfortable with having taken the note, but suspected the meeting would deal with something written in it. Now that he possessed the note, he knew he could handle better the situation. No thanks to Ellie, but he had the trump card with him.

As ordered, a crew of muscled men began sawing and hacking on the front side of the north border. Manny moved his mower to the tall storm-beaten grass after riding to a shallow clearing facing east of the property line around the thicket of trees. There he was able to squeeze through a small area that dumped him in the grassy field. He took the first row of grass slowly choking out his tractor several times over the snarled and tangled rough stalks. It was not an easy decision he had made to rid the barn of its privacy, but his wife was different since moving here. And Manny desperately wanted back the Ellie he had married.

He went row by row wondering if what he was doing was the right thing. When he reached the oak trees near the old barn, his path changed from being straight to circling the trees. But he was unable to get close to their roots for a smooth cut. His motor choked out again with a loud pop just as he finished the farthest tree from the barn. Manny turned the ignition, but restarting was fruitless. It only made a clicking noise.

He jumped from his seat to the ground, grabbing a sling saw to use around the base of the closest tree to him. He would work his way to the barn, hitting around the base of the other dozen or so trees and call it an evening, since he was quite hungry. This time Ellie fooled him and had not come with food as usual.

Swinging his way forward in wide forceful strokes, Manny was four feet away from the tree trunk when he spied a makeshift cross. He put his sling saw down to examine his immediate surroundings. He discovered a mound of dirt with two sticks attached with a leather belt as a marker. He leaped back, realizing that he was standing on top of a grave. Manny pulled the grass growing around the marker up with his bare hands to see if it was the old man who had been controlling in his death by depriving his kin of his grave's location. He saw carved in the vertical stick the name Claudine.

"Humph," Manny strained with surprise. "What in the world?" He questioned the location of somebody else's body being on his land.

His eyes followed the length of the raised dirt, and he made an assumption that it was an adult. Out of nowhere, it hit him. Claudine was the name the attorney mentioned his grandfather wanted to will his new brick house. Manny stooped down to read the dates:

EXPECT SUNSHINE

Born 1/7/30 - Found 6/10/85
Rest in Peace My Love

Manny dropped to his knees. He recognized the long narrow letters as his grandfather's writing from the field notes he had inherited along with the estate papers. He examined the cross closer, seeing a rusty necklace chain with the initial "C" dangling from the belt loop.

He pushed his face into his hand, thinking of all he had discovered here in Chester. Surely, this Claudine was his wife's mother who her note indicated had suffered at the hands of his grandfather, the infamous Mr. Spooky. The Claudine who ran away to save herself, leaving Ellie, was resting in peace. Manny felt sure this was the same lady Ellie wanted so desperately to find when she fled to Chicago.

Rereading the dates, he focused on the empty space, and the fact there was not a date of death. Thinking of Ellie's note, Manny's heart sank believing that the poor buried soul had been there from the very night she had escaped. Years passed as her bones lay exposed right under their noses here in the no-man's land. His grandfather, rest his soul, must have stumbled across her remains one day in the summer of 1985.

***

The body buried was Claudine, Ellie's mother, who had slipped away from George Custer Banks' grip. When all was quiet the night he hit her, she lifted his arms from her shoulders and tipped silently out the door. As the moon and the stars hid under a cloudy sky, she pressed for the abandoned barn. In a fit of tears with a swollen mouth, Claudine ran planning to wait for morning and then get help. Bitten by the briers and dodging limbs she charged through the woods for her freedom. Barely able to see in the dark while jumping over a stump, she hit a root and stumbled headfirst, smashing her head on the large tree trunk. She fell to her death in the middle of the night, having hemorrhaged in the brain. The few seconds that she had blanked in and out she had cried for Ellie. No one heard her pleas in distress.

One summer day in 1985, Mr. Spooky hunted for quail in the tall brush. An aging man with his catch stopped to rest from the heat under the oak tree, and there he witnessed her dried skeleton. He gasped at the shiny gold necklace dangling on the bones near the large root. He was struck with the horror he had done, knowing that she had been there since the night of their fight. He relived that bloody night.

Unable to deal with the truth of that terrible night, it was like he had raised his hand and struck her down. In anguish, Mr. Spooky threw away the birds covered in red from his bullet holes. Wiping his hands, he went into a trance and scampered with the little blood on his palms like it was Claudine's from that night. His mind slipped, and he walked back with his gun held like he was carrying her in his arms. The devastated old man had invited her from the grave to be with him.

It was not until he sat on his porch half-naked that anyone knew his plight. He was seen acting disturbed by his workers who came each month to pick up their pay. But his manner was not taken seriously, since it was a very hot day.

He had continued in a fog puttering around talking to her each day in and day out. Mr. Spooky clenched his destiny with Claudine, acting like she was alive, although he later had buried her in a grave with his bare hands. He did whatever his weak mind said would please her. After a few years, he began the plans to build a brand new house to make his beloved Claudine smile. When Mr. Spooky wanted to ensure her happiness, he went to his lawyer to change his will. Recognizing his feebleness after his request, his attorney had refused to make the change and had him put in a nursing home for complete care. He babbled Claudine while setting his final affairs in order. Mr. Spooky was so tormented by his actions on that night, and she haunted him in his old age like a living ghost until he died, driven crazy.

✳✳✳

Manny could only wonder that Ellie had whined and missed her mother there in the barn while she rested in peace, just a few yards away from Ellie's secret place at the foot of this tree. He thought this special place of Ellie's was a hideaway, which her mother had loved as well. Maybe she had tried to make it to the barn the unfortunate bloody night. Manny wished he knew the truth, but locating the grave of Ellie's mother would provide her some comfort. If her mother had not run off and abandoned her like his wife thought, he had to tell her right away.

Standing up and moving over to collect his sling saw, Manny felt the ground rise and then easily sink under his feet in shorter grass. In the same instant, he slung vigorously and found his grandfather's undisclosed and unmarked gravesite buried next to the only one, who had not left him on the farm. While partially hidden by the tall brush, he outwardly mourned for the first time his grandfather's death.

His selfish act to rid Ellie of her hidden meeting place divulged the last act of his grandfather to be near his beloved Ms. Claudine. Surely, he loved the woman, in the odd way he knew how to express his love, under the disenchantment of eight deserting children. Brought low and humbled, Mr. Spooky was scorned that he had cast a shadow on loving Claudine, having mocked her love for him. He had been unwilling to believe that he was worthy of her love. But in the end, they were together after the years apart while Claudine's body had lain in the wilderness and both were all alone.

Manny tried again to crank his tractor flicking the key, but the starter teased him and droned. A belt had torn or he had blown his engine, so Manny left his ride and followed the same path Ellie had many times home.

✳✳✳

Kent was pronounced dead before Ellie arrived with Officer Zachary. Sonny viewed his son's body with Ellie holding herself up in his arms. She grieved clutching the old man's hand around her waist, not accepting that Kent was gone—forever a missing part of her life. Or was he, when the likes of him flowed as warm blood in a young woman miles away?

"Ellie, there is nothing we can do." Sonny shook her hands, bringing her attention to the present. "I'll take you home." He offered and pulled her away from Kent's side.

Struggling to hold themselves together, they passed the nurses' station. The long hallway seemed dark in the middle of the day as they left the morgue unaware of the eyes that followed them. With broken hearts, Sonny and Ellie made it out through the emergency waiting room to where Zachary wearily waited. The young man, burdened with the sting of taking a life, could not bear to offer his assistance. Too ashamed, the upset police officer stepped aside, hanging his head in sorrow.

A block over, they could hear the evening freight train wheels click clicking on the rails, and the whistle blew loudly. They passed people under umbrellas that covered their heads and saved hairdos in the drizzle before they arrived at Sonny's truck still running with the driver's side door opened. Driving against the path of the sun, they witnessed the remains of a day that neither one ever expected to meet. They had lost Kent.

Had Sonny's prayers of holding onto the land died along with his only son? His mind was painfully locked on Kent and recalling how to get home, not once thinking about his inevitable loss of the land under the Moccasin Pond deal.

CHAPTER ELEVEN

At home, Ellie met Manny on the porch sitting in his rocker with the folding tray in front of him. He was eating leftover meatloaf and mashed potatoes when Sonny stopped the car. A large glass of iced tea and a bigger container of water lined one side of the fragile standing table. He gestured for her to come as he waved at Sonny. After getting out of the vehicle, Ellie bent her head in the passenger window for several minutes, telling the old man something before he drove off.

Manny's mind rested on Claudine's grave. It had disturbed his day. Still puzzled by what he had found, he forgot to invite Sonny to sit on the porch and talk. When he remembered, Sonny had backed up his truck and was aiming for the bend in the dirt road that led to his farm.

"Mr. Vinson hold up!" Manny rose to attention and yelled. In the car circling the yard was a man who had lost all his cares in the world. "We can talk now," Manny shouted, wrapping his hand around a pole at the base of the steps, swinging his body and elevating his voice in an unsuccessful attempt to catch him.

Manny would have to wait to add another piece to his puzzle about Ellie's past life in Chester with the events of the last weeks hammering at his common sense.

"Honey, it's no use," Ellie said, approaching him with an elongated face, very somber.

"What's wrong?" he asked, and was curious for the peculiar fact that Ellie had been riding with Sonny.

He wondered if the meeting Sonny wanted with him had taken place instead with her. Surely, her sterile look was an effort to intercept his right to unscramble what he had recently learned.

Ellie came straight to Manny and buried herself into his arms, saying, "Something terrible just happened."

She shuddered in his embrace as he held her, forgetting the questions brewing on his mind.

"It's alright, honey," Manny consoled his wife. He liked her turning to him to weather her worries. "Whatever it is. We can handle it, Ellie, OK," Manny said, holding her.

Ellie held on to him with both hands to keep her balance coming up the porch steps. "Sonny lost Kent today. He was killed in a shooting," she said stone-faced as her voice was vanishing.

"What!" Manny sat her down in his rocker, and he knelt by her side. "My, I just don't know what to say," he said, very concerned.

Ellie told him about the officer flying up their lane with the news of a prisoner escaping, and in his capture, Kent was shot.

"Is there anything we can do?" he asked, holding her hand to comfort his wife.

Ellie's knotted stomach stirred her thoughts to the Moccasin Pond deal. Her last talk with Kent had revealed his concerns about providing an heir for the Vinson land. He was adamant about his obligation and had made it a mission. She knew now that his mission was hers. She could right the wrong that was thrust upon the Vinsons and her very own life by finding his daughter. The only way she could be at peace was knowing she had tried to find Armanda.

More than ever, Ellie had the strongest reason to look for their daughter. It could make all the difference for a family that she loved dearly. Ellie had to risk Manny's understanding and go to Chicago. She had to find her daughter.

"Manny," Ellie looked into his eyes. "I know you have questions for me since coming to Chester. There are answers. I will give you all of them, but please..." She was scared she was asking too much and hesitated.

The heat of the hottest summer day made her more miserable. Ellie was not sure how to ask or what to explain to Manny. But he was right there with her, hanging on to words, and he spoke first.

"Ellie, do what you have to do. I'll be right here beside you." Manny helped her with a difficult request to leave her husband, temporarily, without a full explanation.

"I need to return to Chicago to handle something I should've a longtime ago," Ellie managed.

"What about the funeral?" Manny reminded her of her friend's right to a proper good-bye. Then he realized that Ellie would search for her adopted daughter and bring her back to her father's burial.

"Oh, I plan to be back before then. If not, I've failed," she said, trying not to fall loose at her seams.

"Honey, there are things I need to tell you," Manny said, keeping the news of her mother's grave, next to his grandfather's final resting place in the brush, to himself.

Contemplating what she could add to Kent's short life and the deaths of their kin found in the grass today, Manny brought sense to Ellie's ways and the defenses that she had built up overtime.

***

A few hours later, Manny drove Ellie fifty miles to Albany for a connection to Chicago via a small chopper. After several stopovers and plane changes, she was back in Chicago. Ellie waited at the arrival's curbside, holding one bag, a backpack, and an upside down smile. In the warm night air, Cousin Mae's stationwagon pulled up to the crowded terminal where Ellie was waving her to stop.

The place was too busy with people moving, pulling small roller bags, carrying flowers or looking lost. Under the circumstances for Ellie, Chicago had lost its luster in spite of the neon advertising signs, the world's best pizza and some of its tallest buildings.

"Bless your heart," Cousin Mae uttered in a hoarse voice with her window rolled down.

Reaching to hug her cousin, she pressed their faces together over the junk mail, fast food trash, and worn stockings littering the front seat.

"Welcome back, young lady," she said to Ellie, who was torn apart and mourning the death of Kent.

She mustered a smile, but was quite depressed thinking of how to accomplish the task that she had pondered during the five-hour ordeal of getting there.

"Thank you, I missed you so much," Ellie managed to say.

She was very tired. Wearily, she sat in the hot car with the single bag on her lap and the backpack, which doubled as a purse, at her feet.

"You remember Kent don't you?" she asked her aging cousin whose temples were lined with a touch of gray peeking from under her night scarf.

"Yes, my dear, your Beau from before you came to live with me from Chester," she said, wondering why Ellie had failed to mention Manny first. "He was a looker, I remember, and a fine young man," she added and now even more curious than before.

"He died today," Ellie bluntly stated, surprising her driver. She swished around in the front seat, trying to find a comfortable spot in the car without air conditioning. "His funeral is on Monday," she gasped.

"Nooo," Cousin Mae sang and then jumped to conclusions about this sudden visit. She belted, "If what I think brings you here, we can turnaround right now, Missy!" Cousin Mae was mad at the thought that the baby given up for adoption would be the next thing Ellie mentioned.

"Cousin Mae, how can you say that?" Ellie asked, getting angry at the day's events.

First, she was detoured from gathering the note from the barn. And later, she ran unexpectedly to Kent's side too late to see him alive or say her peace. Now, this bossy cousin of hers, who thought of the whole adoption thing in the first place, was acting funny. Cousin Mae's unwillingness to give Ellie the information she needed to begin her search would be costly. Her precious time was ticking away with each minute she lost, begging.

Apologetically and cordially, Ellie rephrased her outburst. "I need your help, it's really important to tell Armanda that her father is dead," she said and waited for a response.

Cousin Mae drove on the expressway ignoring Ellie while looking for a place to turnaround and take her back to the airport.

"Please, please," Ellie cried. "It's not for me, it's for Kent and his dad."

Unconvinced, Cousin Mae slowed down to take an exit ramp.

"What are you doing? No!" Ellie shouted. "You have to help me. I know you handled everything. You know where Armanda is," she pleaded.

The car rolled to a near stop at an empty gas station, and Cousin Mae made a U-turn, still ignoring Ellie. She had no intention of getting involved in breaking the law.

"Just let me out!" Ellie shouted, "I'll find her all by myself."

"Child, this would be breaking the law to give you that information. Do you know that?" Cousin Mae asked.

She put her concerns on the table as she drove, checking for the interstate sign in the opposite direction of home. Moving as fast as she could, the front seat junk rustled about from the wind whipping through the windows.

"Will you have the least bit of sympathy for a dead father who never knew his child? Shouldn't she see him for once—in dead flesh?" Ellie screamed out of control and desperate to get her Cousin Mae to cooperate.

Undaunted, Cousin Mae wheeled the car onto the expressway one mile from the airport. Ellie saw her hope vanishing with the determined and once reliable cousin being very unresponsive. Traffic was backed up in all lanes going to the airport causing them to creep at a snail's pace. No one said another word, and they moved closer away from any chance of Ellie finding Armanda.

Silence hung in the barrier between them.

"Two hours, Cousin Mae." Ellie broke the truce. "Two hours were all you gave me to make a decision that I've had to live with, not you."

Her statement tugged Cousin Mae's heart and reminded her that it had been very unfair to the scared teenager. But it would have broken the deal she had made for Ellie and the newborn child. It was her business to place babies and Ellie's was making quota. She had treated the whole affair as a job when it was an emotional disaster for Ellie.

"Ellie, I'm so sorry for Kent, you, and the baby," she said with genuine sadness. "I don't work with placing babies anymore. It got to me. So, how am I going to get the information you need?" She questioned her ability to be of any help.

"You knew the family didn't you? I heard you say their name once. It slipped when you were talking one day just like they were friends or acquaintances of yours." Ellie said it very sure she was recalling correctly. For years, she had racked her brain for every clue possible about who adopted her child and had tried to find her.

"You're right. It was a lady from my sister's church in Evanston," Cousin Mae remembered, looking a little uncomfortable. "I think they changed their membership several years ago. Honey, we're running out of means to settle this," she said.

After clouding the urgent situation with doubt, Cousin Mae circled the airport exit ramp and headed home, once again. Turning back on the expressway, traffic coasted at the speed limit. A breeze cooled them and rustled the front seat's trash.

"I'm thinking about it. I believe they moved from where we took the baby." Cousin Mae said, trying to remember.

"Do you recalled where?" Ellie pounced.

"I don't even remember their names," she responded to her thoughts rather than Ellie.

Cousin Mae was visibly uncomfortable, and her heart was pierced with guilt. After all, the baby was family, not just some number on a sheet of paper and an extra zero in her paycheck.

"We can go first thing in the morning to the home where I placed the baby." Cousin Mae said and she made peace with her part in the deal.

"Thank you for any help," Ellie sighed.

She was ready to sleep lying down rather than sitting up on a cramped airplane as she had on the last leg of her trip.

The next morning, Cousin Mae made a vegetable omelet for breakfast with biscuits and gravy from scratch. Ellie woke up with vivid memories of her first years here in Chicago. She had shared many good times with the plump lady in the kitchen who rescued her from Mr. Spooky. Cousin Mae understood Ellie's loneliness for her mother and had been someone she could lean on.

Ellie recalled the first time that her true pal and trusted confidant met Manny on their second date. Cousin Mae liked him so much she had proclaimed he would be her husband someday. The threesome had often played Scrabble and Twenty-One late into many nights as Cousin Mae drank hard liquor, and the two of them drank ginger ales.

Her room was very much like when she left. Twin beds without headboards were propped against a deep gold wall opposite the door. Bright white twisted fringe bedspreads dressed both. Extra colorful pillows and several stuffed animals sat on each bed. The tiny stuffed ones were on hers, and the larger characters laid on the spare. A cherry wood chest of drawers was centered between the windows with the same curtains and pulls when she had lived in the room. One live green plant was suffering on the windowsill.

The door creaked and Ellie raised up.

"Are you up?" Cousin Mae asked, poking her head in. Ellie heard the familiar question that her elderly cousin had asked early each Saturday morning when she was a resident of the two-bedroom apartment.

"Yes, I'm on my way in a minute," Ellie said and got out of bed. She grabbed a robe hanging on a hook on the back of the door as her barefoot touched the cool tile floor. Ellie washed her faced and slid to the breakfast table very hungry.

"Yummy," she stuck the first fork full of hot omelet with melted cheese in her mouth. Lots of mushrooms, green peppers, onions plus tomatoes were wedged in the eggs smothered in American cheese. "It's just like old times. Thank you," Ellie told her cousin and gave her a shove on the shoulder. She laughed realizing she had not enjoyed the hardy feeling in days.

"Honey, we've got a job ahead of us. You gotta be back by Monday for the funeral. Let me grace this table so we can start." Cousin Mae prayed a long spiel short of asking for a miracle.

Ellie ravaged her old favorites she had missed.

"This is so good," she munched.

"We'll go to Evanston first and see if they still live in the same house. If so, it's up to you to talk to the girl. Now, I'm not an expert on this type of stuff anymore, but the majority of these adopted children resent their birth parents butting into their lives." Cousin Mae tried to prepare Ellie for the chance of a letdown if they found her daughter. "There are no guarantees. You can't make

163

things happen that aren't supposed to," she continued, eating and talking at the same time.

"I understand what you're saying." Ellie fished in her scattered, now cold, omelet for mushrooms, thinking Armanda had to listen to her.

***

In Evanston, they studied a raggedy city map used during Cousin Mae's agency placement days while sitting on a tree-lined street in a nice neighborhood. Cousin Mae had looted under her seat and produced it before she pulled from her assigned parking space at the rear of her apartment building.

"Alright, we're close. I see where we turn on the next block, go three streets and make a right. Then the house should be on the left." Cousin Mae traced the route with her finger and seconded her own observation as accurate.

"How do you feel?" she asked, looking at a placid Ellie.

They began their journey with numerous papers, old mail and dropped French fries riding along, and witnessing the two muddled with fixing what happened more than twenty years ago.

"I'm OK," Ellied replied.

"We're in this together, so don't forget that." Cousin Mae reached over and patted Ellie's thigh for a vote of confidence.

The stationwagon dragged on the street where she had closed the deal and handed Ellie's little baby girl to the well-to-do family. They peered out in the pristine neighborhood, wondering what would happen if they found Armanda. Cousin Mae cruised to the curbside and parked between two cars in front of the family's house. Someone was home.

Taking a deep breath, Ellie did not have the nerve to get out. Her palms sweated.

"Cousin Mae, I'm scared," Ellie said with her door still shut.

"Awe, girl, get out and take care of your business," she rattled off at a pitiful looking Ellie. "Now, we didn't come here for this backsliding," she fussed.

Like a busybody, Cousin Mae stepped onto the brick sidewalk to make her way to the storm door.

Ellie watched Cousin Mae haul away from the car in a hiked up dress showing the top of her socks that she wore with nursing shoes. At the door, Cousin Mae put her hands on her hips as soon as it opened.

A timid lady with gray hair and a slim build stood behind a locked glass storm door. She made hand gestures. Ellie could not make out what was being said. She momentarily took her eyes off Cousin Mae, surveying the car's trash and when Ellie looked back, Cousin Mae was heading for the car.

Opening the door and slamming it shut, she said, "They don't live there anymore. They haven't in years." Cousin Mae adjusted her seatbelt, "Baby, you know Armanda is grown now. She isn't likely to live with the parents anyway," she said, borrowing time to think.

"What did the lady say? Did she know where they moved?" Ellie cross-examined Cousin Mae.

"Calm down," Cousin Mae waved at Ellie to lean back.

"She said the previous owners who had one daughter moved further East to Howell Street. She took some mail over one day years ago and could not remember the house number, but she recalled it being a green house. The only green one in the six hundred block." Cousin Mae reported her investigation.

"We've got to try," Ellie barked.

"We?" Cousin Mae repeated. "Feels more like me than we." She forced the words for Ellie to get her point. She was under pressure with such little information.

Cousin Mae put the car in drive and went to the stop sign where she pulled out her map. After reading it, Cousin Mae kept her insight to herself, since Ellie had proven she was along for the ride.

They cruised to Howell Street and spotted a green house fading with age. Cousin Mae continued the distance of the wide street and made a wheelie at the end of the six hundred block.

"We're here, you go this time," she said to Ellie as she parked near the mailbox in front of the only green house.

"I will." Ellie jumped out and walked halfway up the driveway lined with thick monkey grass.

Getting closer to the door, she wondered had the adopted parents changed Armanda's name. Ellie continued her way looking down and intentionally avoided stepping on the breaks in the concrete slab, which lead to the house with a small glass window in the center of the door.

Nervously, she rang the doorbell. No one answered. Ellie pushed the bell a second time. The sun blasted the front of the house where she stood, making her hot. Still no one came. Ellie looked back at Cousin Mae in the car who was gesturing with a balled fist to knock on the door. She hit hard in the air at an imaginary door with one hand as she dangled an old newspaper in the other. Slightly annoyed at Cousin Mae's arrogance, Ellie put her hands in her pockets and waited. After a minute, she knocked on the door, and someone opened it.

"Hello, is Armanda home?" Ellie asked like she was a neighborhood child soliciting a playmate.

"She doesn't live here anymore," the neat looking lady said.

"Are you her mother?" Ellie stuttered, knowing she was stirring off course with her curiosity of who had held her baby daughter each night that she had not.

"Yes, I'm Armanda's mother," the lady peering out said, becoming hesitant and uncomfortable. "Why do you want my daughter?" the not-so-nice lady added.

Ellie, off guard, blurted, "I know her birth father died." Sweat rolled down her chest in her cotton blouse and trickled to her stomach as she stood in full sunlight.

"She has a living father, my husband." The owner of the faded green house closed her door to an inch, ready to slam it.

"Please, I only want Armanda to know that he didn't get a chance with her," Ellie pleaded. When the lady huffed, she knew she had over stepped her boundary.

"No, she doesn't need him." Armanda's adopted mother slammed the door shut in Ellie's red face.

Cousin Mae could see the exchange had been too long for anything of worth to come out of it, so she would go easy on Ellie. As Ellie returned to the stationwagon, she passed expensive cars in the driveway in an even nicer neighborhood.

"Get in, it's alright," Cousin Mae eyed Ellie and threw her newspaper in the backseat when Ellie closed her door. She cranked the car as it struggled to catch. "What did you find out?" Cousin Mae continued, pacifying Ellie who looked like she had met the devil.

"Armanda moved away," Ellie gasped.

"When?"

"She didn't say."

"And you didn't ask," Cousin Mae said in a frustrated tone, forgetting to be supportive.

"Well it's not over until the fat lady sings," Ellie spoke, sitting up tall showing confidence that she was determined.

"So what are you trying to say? I'm supposed to sing now," Cousin Mae said, being smart as she pointed the vehicle to downtown Chicago.

Time was ticking away. Ellie was as close to finding Armanda as she was when her arriving airplane had touched down on the runway. Desperate to locate Armanda, her mind was racing.

"What if she just moved, and the post office has her new address?" Ellie quipped.

Cousin Mae turned her head away from moving traffic momentarily and looked at Ellie. With a blank face she informed her in a matter-of-fact way, "Then the post office has it, not you or me!" She raised her voice and chided, "For crying out loud, Ellie, help me!" Cousin Mae was frustrated with Ellie's business.

Thirty minutes later, the car chuckled into the alley behind her apartment with two tired souls wondering what to do next. Ellie went ahead of Cousin Mae to the door and waited as the she puffed her way with the key.

"Relax," Cousin Mae said, twisting the key and giving the door a small kick with her knee. "We will think of something."

She walked in stepping on more mail that had been slipped in the mail drop. The stressed older lady's dress rose up as she bent down showing her back thighs to Ellie. With her arms crossed, Ellie waited to get inside to crash on the sofa. She was exhausted. Cousin Mae blocked her out while picking up the newsletters, bills and numerous catalogs. Her house was full of unread newspaper and magazines.

"I've got it!" she yelled, like she had won the lottery with blood rushing to her head while stooping.

It scared Ellie, and she jumped in the apartment, bumping Cousin Mae out of her way.

"My good friend, Wayne, works at the post office. Maybe it's breaking the rules, but he can tell us where Armanda moved," she said excitedly. "That's it, it could work." Cousin Mae looked at a tired Ellie who was on the sofa with her feet on the table.

"Yes, let's call him now," Ellie chimed.

"Are you crazy?" Cousin Mae barked, "He's at work. Someone could overhear our call and report it. We have to be careful and wait until he gets home."

Not the least bit satisfied with her day, Ellie proposed, "Or we can call him and have him call us on a pay telephone or cell phone. We don't have time to waste."

She picked up the telephone half buried on the sofa and waved it, ready for immediate action. Ellie ranted, "He has got to get started right away. Tomorrow is Friday, and they're probably closed on Saturday."

"Hand me the telephone book," Cousin Mae suggested and looked up Wayne's work number. "Let's see he's at the downtown branch."

She pressed her finger steadily under each printed number of the post office listings until she found the one she wanted. They were under the gun to cover as much ground today as possible, so she obliged Ellie and dialed the numbers.

"Hello, may I speak to Wayne in operations?" Cousin Mae asked. "He's not in?" she repeated disappointedly, "When will he be back?" Cousin Mae inquired, hoping to get an answer from the person on the other end that sounded too busy. "It's really important that he gets this message as soon as possible," she told the lady who was chewing bubble gum. "Thank you." Cousin Mae hung up the telephone not encouraged.

"Keep thinking, Ellie," she said, resting next to Ellie on the sofa.

She tried several times to put her feet on the tabletop, but could not raise her legs up high enough or long enough to reach it.

Ellie took a pillow and laid her head on it.

"What about someone from her parent's old church?" Ellie asked, thinking out loud. "They may know Armanda personally, and we wouldn't need Wayne to jeopardize his job," she planned.

"OK, you're on to something, let me think. Well, there is one thing," Cousin Mae said pitifully. "I kinda made the preacher's wife mad after taking over the women's ministry."

Then she sheepishly recanted, "The whole conference knows about it. I can't go to them for information."

Cousin Mae never ceased to amaze Ellie. Hearing her cousin squirm through telling the story, Ellie sat dumbfounded.

"But, Wayne is one of my best friends. He will help us," Cousin Mae said, pointing her finger like she was counting her blessings. "Child, let's get something to eat. What do you want for dinner?" She offered not worried at all.

Ellie was not hungry and hunched her shoulders. She was worried with her mind still tackling a solution. Her cousin fixed their dinner and read the newspaper while waiting for Wayne to call. Ellie fell asleep, thinking of what to do. At sundown, Cousin Mae woke her up and set a plate of black beans and rice on the table. Under the pressure of finding Armanda, Ellie had lost her appetite and pushed the meal aside.

It was after working hours, and they assumed the sassy secretary had failed to tell Wayne about their call. Cousin Mae pacified Ellie and left a message on his home recorder, so there was nothing to do but wait. Ellie fell back asleep, worrying. Every time the telephone rang she raised up only to see Cousin Mae's hand moving a finger across the neck, signaling that it was not the call they were waiting for.

Snoozing off and on, Ellie was ready for bed when the late night news was coming on. Her body ached under the stress. As soon as her feet hit the floor, the telephone buzzed. Wayne was finally calling.

"Where have you been?" Cousin Mae said not a bit interested in his answer, and she went straight to business.

Anxious after he finally called, Ellie paced on the worn carpet.

"I need a big favor," Cousin Mae pouted. "I need you to locate someone for me. Can you help me if I have the last known address of the person?" she hurriedly asked on Ellie's behalf, giving him the old address.

Wayne was not pleased with her request. He told her about the rules and how he could lose his job if the post office ever found out. Cousin Mae listened. And when he was through complaining, she kindly said, "Be careful."

"I'm sorry I can't," Wayne said sympathetically. "You understand, don't you?"

"Sure, I do," she said and burst into a sudden fit of tears. Cousin Mae's boisterous voice made her cry sound life threatening.

It startled Wayne. He had known her most of his life, and she had never dropped a tear since high school that he could remember. She cried louder when he tried to interrupt her.

"Hey, are you OK, Mae?" he asked several times as she threw her fit, acting. "Alright, alright I'll see what I can do. But I can't promise anything will turn up, you hear," he said annoyed and waited for the noise to subside. When she stopped to blow her nose, he said, "Good night."

Ellie observed her cousin bawling and wondered what was really happening before her eyes, as she, too, had never seen her cousin cry. Ellie owed Cousin Mae the world and got up to get them glasses of water. When she returned, Cousin Mae gave her plenty of hope that Wayne would call first thing in the morning with an address for Armanda. The two drank their glasses of water like it was champagne and went to bed for a good night's sleep.

On Friday morning, Ellie puttered about the apartment with her cousin, catching up on the happenings in Chicago as they waited for his call. By noon, he had not called and Cousin Mae fumed with the letdown. Ellie kept talking and hoping he would soon as time slipped away.

Cousin Mae dialed again the post office's number and asked for operations, "Good afternoon, is Wayne in?" she asked. "What, you're kidding me. He didn't go in to work today at all!" Cousin Mae squawked into the mouthpiece. "Gee, thank you, good-bye," she ended the call.

When she hung up, Ellie was at her side.

"Can you believe this? Wayne didn't even go to work at the post office, today. He took the day off! We're wasting time," Cousin Mae said in disbelief.

"Is Wayne home? What's going on?" Ellie asked out loud as Cousin Mae called his home number.

Her fingers punched each number hard.

"Hello," she said to an answering machine.

Turning to Ellie, she said, "We've been stood up, Ellie." She shook her head, looking at Ellie now sitting with her arms folded.

"We must go back to that house," Ellie proposed.

"And get the door slammed harder in your face?"

"You speak to her this time," Ellie offered, not giving up on locating her daughter.

"Well, she saw me in the car. She's on guard now," Cousin Mae said. "No, that will not work."

"Let's go and wait to see if Armanda visits her adopted parents. If she is still in the city maybe she goes over there regularly. That's better than sitting here waiting. Armanda isn't coming here," Ellie snapped.

"OK, we can do that," Cousin Mae agreed. She snatched off her headscarf and said, "Wayne has pulled a fast one on me. Let's go, Missy girl."

Walking out the door, she patted her short Afro into place. Ellie beat her to the hallway and held the elevator door open for them.

Under an hour, they made it to the street with the green house and parked on the opposite side. While waiting, they fussed and talked—and fussed and talked. It was about four o'clock when the ladies decided that their chances of finding Armanda were slim.

"Cousin Mae, please call somebody at your old office and see if they can help us." Hot and irritably, Ellie whined.

She handed her a cell phone she had sat on in the seat.

"Girl, you're gonna make me run up my bill," Cousin Mae said as Ellie twitched with frustration.

Cousin Mae thrashed in the pile of junk and papers, locating her lost personal telephone book. She searched the pages for the best contact. Dialing, she eyed the house across the street with the green door.

"Hello, is Odell in today?" Cousin Mae asked, knowing there was a huge chance her old counterpart was in the field making her numbers. "Well, have her call me at this number," she repeated them twice and hit the "End" button.

"Look," Ellie said, pointing at a lady coming out the green house.

Ellie wanted the snooty lady who had slammed the door in her face to lead them to Armanda.

Ellie anxiously mouthed like a hypnotist, "Get into the car, get into the car." She did. "Let's go. She might lead us to Armanda." Ellie spoke fast and excitedly.

Cousin Mae waited for the meticulous dressed woman to get a headstart and then they followed. The vehicle they tagged slowed and stopped at a highrise building near the Northwestern University campus. Armanda's adopted mother exited the car and once on the building's steps she pressed a button on the outside, which she kept her finger on while leaning forward to speak into a vent.

A short distance away, both Cousin Mae and Ellie got out of the stationwagon and went to a newsstand under a big tree where its bulging roots had split the sidewalk. Ellie made sure that she did not step on the cracks. The news bend was tilted on the uneven pavement, and her cousin used it to rest on.

"I'm here," the lady said to someone who answered through the small vent and entered in the doors.

They hoped it was Armanda. Her adopted mom went in and the automatic door closed.

Ellie and Cousin Mae rushed to it, missing their chance to get inside. Through the finger-smudged glass, they could see a row of mailboxes with names printed in block style fonts. The tall perfect looking woman got in the elevator. To get inside the building, they needed a key for access or someone to buzz them in. No one manned the front desk. With no possible options, they waited outside. So close to likely finding Armanda, Ellie painfully camped on the steps, watching and waiting for someone to enter or leave the building. She was sure they would find Armanda here.

Cousin Mae legs moved ten steps forward and then ten steps backwards on the sidewalk, pacing. Folding her arms after waiting ten minutes, Ellie watched the legs sprint by her up the steps.

Cousin Mae started beating on the door, "Let me in!" she yelled at no one.

"Stop that! You're going to get us arrested," Ellie proposed, looking inside the empty corridor. "Shhhh," Ellie frowned as two young students stepped out of the elevator carrying books. Behind them were a young woman in sweats, and the other, the snooty old lady they had followed. The fancy lady stood a minute and they kissed the other's cheek before the young lady got back in the elevator.

"Cousin Mae, she's coming toward the door. You get on the sidewalk and slip in like an ordinary resident while I get back to the car."

Cousin Mae snapped back, "Why don't you slip in?"

"What if she remembers me?" Ellie said, and begin to move toward the car.

She looked over her shoulders and saw Cousin Mae was standing in the same spot, being difficult.

Ellie tapped her watch and waved her to the door before saying, "Hurry."

"OK, I'm on it." Cousin Mae squeaky nursing shoes beat the pavement a short distance down on the sidewalk.

When Armanda adopted mom came to the entrance Cousin Mae swung up the steps in time to catch the opened door. She was on the inside. Once the lady drove off, Ellie got out of the car and went inside. Cousin Mae opened the door wide for her, triggering the automatic buzzer.

They gave each other high fives, giggling at their small success. Inside the corridor smelled like a library where Ellie read the mailboxes. The huge lobby had hard vinyl furnishings that decorated the bottom floor from end to end. Tripping over her feet, Ellie looked for Armanda's name. Cousin Mae went behind her checking. At the end of the boxes, they stood with their hands on their hips; not one person was listed as Armanda.

"Wait," Cousin Mae said and backed up to a box that had "A. Fairweather" written on it. "That's it. I remember now the family's name was Fairweather."

"Oh, thank you," Ellie grabbed her cousin and danced in a hug, believing they had found Armanda.

CHAPTER TWELVE

*O*n Friday, Officer Zachary Glasser marched into the police station and turned in his badge to his commanding officer as Chester mourned one of its favorite sons, Kent Vinson.

"Zachary, it was an accident. You don't have to do this," his boss said.

With red, strained eyes, Zachary offered his two uniforms bought on an advance against his first paycheck, without blinking.

"I can't do it anymore. It's not for me," he said.

Leaning on the counter, he found the energy to empty the bag of police stuff, caps, boots, and a windbreaker. He jostled last from the bottom of the bag his official hat. The same one he had a difficult time in officer training school learning how to hold when a superior was present.

"We don't blame you. It unfortunately comes with the territory. You were only doing your job, young man," he said.

The formally dressed officer with extra stripes for 20 full years of service looked at Zachary, standing wearily just three months on the beat. He put his hands on the returns.

Zachary ignored his comments and continued to spread his gear on the table.

"You gotta put this out of your mind, or it will get to you." He offered to shake Zachary's hand.

Zachary stopped what he was doing and shook his hand.

"We got the prisoner back behind bars," his superior officer said, gesturing his understanding.

Zachary was weak with pain and unforgiving of himself.

"If there is anything I can do to help you, please ask me. We think a lot of you and your courage here at the station," his old boss said sincerely.

His final words hit the back of Zachary's neck as he left the police station empty-handed.

Six months ago Zachary was a shining star in the small town, a young college graduate doing well running his family farm. Then the land was snatched away, and his life turned upside down. This week, he hit another low as he tussled with taking the life of an innocent man.

He had seen Kent's body lying in the casket and every part of him ached while staring at his victim in a dark suit with his hands crossed on the front lapels. It was a terrible thing to witness, let alone cause. Quite wearily, he got in his vehicle and drove to the nursing home to see his mother.

He tipped his baseball cap at the nurse's station and sneaked down the left wing, which housed his mother who was his best friend. He passed the doors decorated with shiny nameplates like it was really someone's home.

At her door, he closed his eyes for a moment. Zachary tucked his shirttail in his pants before he peered in her partially opened door and went inside. His mother sat at the window, expecting sunshine on a cloudy day.

"Hey, how you doing today?" Zachary said, causing her to jump at the sudden break in the sterile silence of a TV that was soundless but blinked when the pictures changed.

"Baby, I'm fine, but I want to go home. I'll cook you a meal real soon," she said in a humble voice while playing with the only plant that she had—a philodendron from him.

There was no home for the Glassers. Hearing her chatter about home, he knew that his mother had blocked out their foreclosure. They had lost everything, including her pots and pans.

"Give me a hug," he said and wrapped his arms tightly around his mother.

He wanted to cry, but his tears were all dried out from a full day of suffering the unfortunate consequences of Wednesday's shooting.

"Ma, I need to tell you something that I've put off for two days." He wished to spare her. "It's a big mess. I shot a man to death, and I quit the force. I can't do it anymore," he said, hanging his head while rubbing his hands on his face.

The room smelled like medicine. The same odor came in with him from the hall as he passed people with a young boy pushing an old man in a wheelchair. With his arms wrapped tightly around his mother, they stood in the quiet except the sound of feet sliding in house shoes outside her door as some poor soul dragged along.

"Son, I heard it wasn't your fault," she uttered and patted his back. "If you carry this too long, child, you will be right here with me, and I want to go home," she said as he looked in her face, which showed more age than he had ever noticed before.

His mother was letting the loss of the farm eat at her. He felt cursed with all the bad that had blown their way. Zachary did not know where else that she could call home. Her bills were already thirty days past due.

***

Sonny had visited the funeral home each day since Kent's angels took him to glory, and today would be no different. He dressed in the familiar dark garbs. He fed himself oatmeal and toast for breakfast like Kent would have and headed out in the newest truck by himself. Sonny rolled by a freshly picked cotton field as his truck slowly pressed the ruts in the worn tire trails of folks who had brought food and condolences to him. Huge white piles of packed cotton were dumped neatly on the ground in perfect rectangle shapes.

His hired help continued faithfully their duties of harvesting the crops. On the other side of his field, men were shaking peanuts and hauling the trailers into the grading bends.

Sonny was all alone making a right turn out of his property onto the main county road when Sprewell Jr. blocked him. Seeing him, Sonny thought about the Moccasin Pond deal and pulled over, dizzy.

Sprewell Jr., a pint sized man with white hair and overalls, got out of his truck with a rifle rack on its rear window and stood in the middle of the road staring at him.

"Don't you think we need to talk?" he asked, chewing on a whittled stick.

Sonny's head hurt, and he was unable to focus on his foe that came to rubber-stamp their deal.

"I'm in no shape to deal with you right now." Sonny gasped and cranked his truck.

His engine roared. He gunned the gas, but his tires spun in the mud.

"My daddy told your daddy that this day would come. I'm sorry about your loss, but we have a deal." He shuffled in his hands the yellowed stained contract. "I just want to make sure we're straight on what's supposed to happen," he spoke waving the paper in the air. "I want to warn you that we mean to collect free and clear when you gone, so we just as well make the final arrangements," Sprewell Jr. said, thinking he would likely outlive Sonny.

"Man, y'all can have this land. Right now I want to bury my son, so get out of my way," Sonny mustered.

"When are we setting the Quitclaim Deed to say Sprewell?" he asked, showing little respect for the dead.

Sonny grew angry at his enemy's timing with blocking his way and bringing up the land. Sonny had a right to mourn in peace.

"Tell you what, as soon as the funeral is over you come by, and I'll sign over the deed," Sonny choked. "Now, move out of my way!" he ordered him.

Sprewell Jr. took the stick out of his mouth and spat on the ground before he slowly climbed back in his truck and drove on.

On his way to see his dead son, the mourning father gunned his truck off the soft shoulder back on to the road, visibly shaken by the Moccasin Pond deal. Feeling like King Solomon, it was all now meaningless and someone else would enjoy the fruits of his labor. After pulling his truck into the well-traveled ruts, Sonny edged on thinking, "so be it." It took him longer than usual to travel the short distance to town.

His face was flushed when he entered the funeral home to see Kent's body, again. People shook his hand or nodded their heads as he dragged in and passed them like a stiff statue. The organ was playing a stale chord of sad music. A full spread of the town's best cooking lined a long table in the foyer. His Prince Hall Mason brothers busily prepared the wake for a crowd gathering in the funeral home, including Manny. Plenty of strangers patted Sonny on the back as he stood beside the casket with his knuckles to his chin. Minnie Jean was camped solidly near the foot of it, wearing a bun.

"Sir," Manny spoke and stood to Sonny's right while waiting to be acknowledged.

"Yes," Sonny said, facing the distinguished and familiar voice.

"Ellie and I are ready to be of any assistance we can to you as a neighbor and friend," Manny kindly offered. "Just ask and we'll do it."

"Well, I had intended to speak to you about something. I know this is not the best place or time, but it will never be. I had mentioned this to Kent and he really didn't think it was necessary, but it is," Sonny said, walking Manny over to a corner.

Manny worried that this had to do with Ellie and wished the old man would confront him at another time. He was very uncomfortable discussing Ellie now that Kent had passed. Their secret meetings in the barn were over, and Kent posed no threat to his marriage. Manny wanted his Ellie, but he never fathomed the circumstance by which he would win her back.

"I've been meaning to ask you about..." Sonny stopped and coughed.

Manny grew nervous watching Sonny stumble with his thoughts.

"About considering working our land," Sonny said, making his request like Kent was still alive. Aware of how it sounded, Sonny corrected himself, and said, "I mean working my land. I'm too old and my wings are clipped with Kent dying so young." Sonny spoke into space, "...leaving me suddenly."

He hoped that Manny would take him seriously. Gravely, distracted by his last son's death his heart was no longer in the land.

Manny was tricked by his own imagination and hardly had heard Sonny finish before he offered. "We can work it out. Sure we can."

He wanted out of the now over crowded room where a line of well wishers was forming to see Sonny. The place was noisy with chatter, as a long beat jarred endlessly in the organ music. Manny shook Sonny's hand intending to leave space for the next person, but he stopped and asked a question that had been on his mind since Wednesday, "Do you remember Claudine?"

"Of course I do, that was Ellie's mother," Sonny said after hearing a name he had not heard in years. "Where is Ellie? I called the other day but the telephone just rang."

"She went out of town, but she'll be back for the funeral," Manny said. "Sir, we'll talk later. God Bless you." He navigated the crowd and left, having confirmed that Claudine was Ellie's mother.

✱✱✱

The mailbox number for A. Fairweather was 740, which Ellie interpreted as apartment number forty on the seventh floor of the highrise.

"Cousin Mae." Ellie eyes sparkled in disbelief that they could be so close.

"Ellie," she said and pulled her by the collar to get moving.

"OK, OK," Ellie scampered to the elevator behind her cousin who had rushed in first.

The closet-sized space carried them floor by floor as the red light jumped to the numbers of each, cruising silently to the fifth. It opened. A boy and his dog entered. The very frisky animal wagged his tail shedding hair as he played with his owner and hungrily licked Cousin Mae's shoe. "Bing," the elevator chimed and coasted to the seventh floor. Ellie pushed Cousin Mae off who was about to tell the little boy a mouth full.

The elevator opened to an arrow indicating that apartment number 740 was to their right. The hallway's air was fresher and they stepped onto alternating blue-and-green block carpet. A large mirror above a narrow table was on the opposite wall where they exited. Ellie walked the hall, taking wide steps ahead of Cousin Mae. She read the numbers until she faced the sleek brown door with the number 740 above a peeping hole.

"What are you going to say?" Cousin Mae whispered to Ellie when she caught up to her.

"I'm telling her the truth," Ellie shushed her.

"Now remember what I said that, sometimes adopted..." Cousin Mae shut off instantly when Ellie's hand covered her mouth stifling the words she was trying to utter.

Cousin Mae lifted Ellie's hand from her lips, surprised. Knowing Ellie was not ready, she knocked loudly on the door and stood back against the wall, leaving it all for Ellie to handle.

Ellie could not believe they carried on like children as the door opened to a young woman saying, "Mom you forgot this." She was holding a blooming, deep purple African violet in a small ceramic pot.

"Oh, hello, you're not my Mom," she said startled.

Ellie stared speechless.

"May, I help you?" she asked, still holding the flower.

"I'm looking for Armanda," Ellie said, trying to find her features in the pretty face.

"That's me," she answered.

Armanda had a beautiful voice. With a great accent and depth, it gave Ellie pleasure for a moment. She was every bit of what Ellie had imagined the tiny bundle she held for two hours would have grown to look like. Armanda was Ellie's height with Kent's forehead and nose. She wore bangs with a chin length bob.

"My name is Ellie. I came to tell you," Ellie said as she saw the joy in Armanda's face melt while smelling a fruity perfume.

"Oh, you're the person my Mother mentioned who came to her house talking about my birth father," Armanda pounced. "It can't be true because my adoption papers said my birth parents were dead," she said, talking fast and running her words together.

She was fearful of the slightest urge it could be true.

Ellie lips curled as she looked at Cousin Mae out of her peripheral vision. Cousin Mae was pressed flat against the wall, squirming. For over twenty years, she had hidden that one small fact.

Armanda looked scared dressed in blue sweats with the flower squeezed in the crook of her right arm. She had one hand on the doorknob and her foot against the door, leaving a six-inch crack.

"Please, hear me out," Ellie prayed.

"I think you better go before I call the police," Armanda said and pushed the door almost shut.

"I'm your mother, and if you want to ever see your father before he's buried, listen to me!" Ellie shouted tearfully as her eyes darted the hallway for anyone coming.

Armanda pushed the door to close it, but Ellie pushed back while begging her to just listen.

"You're not my real mother," she repeated, staring into Ellie's eyes when it clicked that the eyes were hers. The fat cheeks were hers, and the bushy eyebrows.

The door sprang open and Armanda backed up a step. Ellie saw her giving in and decided to make her more comfortable that she was telling the truth.

Relaxing a bit, Ellie quoted, "I know where every birthmark is on your body—the small of your back has an hourglass shape on it, and your left leg a round clock missing the six o'clock hour on the back of your calf." Ellie breathed hard, rushing the words to get Armanda's attention.

"No, stay outside!" Armanda shouted, confused.

"I'm sorry we have to meet this way, but there hasn't been a day that I haven't thought about you and how I gave you up." Ellie was careful with her daughter. "Your father was innocent in this adoption. He died not knowing you were born."

Armanda listened as Ellie confessed, "I'm the one to blame, so I needed to locate you more for him." Ellie raced her words to get the whole story out.

"Why? Why? Leave me alone just like you did for twenty-two years," Armanda spoke firmly, perspiring.

"I have to tell you your father will be buried on Monday, and his dad needs you there. He has no one. Please, just for one day for the funeral." Ellie pleaded not sure she was reaching Armanda now. "We live in Chester, Georgia. The funeral is at New Salem Missionary Baptist Church on Monday. I leave on the first flight Sunday morning to..."

Cousin Mae's cell phone rang loudly and distracted Ellie before she finished. Armanda saw that there were two of them, and she stopped listening.

Cousin Mae dug in her big purse and answered it whispering, "Hello, Odell."

"I will not go anywhere!" Armanda shouted. "The papers said no parents."

"Listen to me, please," Ellie said forcefully.

"I'm sorry, you have to go!" Armanda slammed the door.

Ellie hollered back with her nose tip to the door, "There will be a ticket for you at the lost and found counter." It was silent.

Emotionally drained, Ellie stood helplessly. Then she hit the wall hard, breaking a fingernail. Nothing and no one stirred including Cousin Mae who was still pressed against the wall, holding her cell phone in mid air.

✷✷✷

At the apartment, an exhausted Ellie flung the door open as Cousin Mae twisted the key in the knob. She mindlessly threw herself on the sofa with mixed matched pillows. They were quiet with conflict between them in the air. Ellie continued to ignore Cousin Mae as she had the whole trip back. Her equally stubborn cousin would not bother to speak either and switched out of the room to the kitchen to check her messages.

"Wayne called," she yelled.

"So what!" Ellie spewed back.

"He's got Armanda's address," she snickered, "Just like we asked."

Cousin Mae had a smile on her face, knowing she wanted to see him this weekend.

"We did our best, Ellie," Cousin Mae said as she strutted back to the sitting room and flopped next to Ellie on the sofa.

"Here, you want to call your husband?" She offered Ellie the telephone.

With a splitting headache, Ellie took it and went to her bedroom, knowing she would return empty-handed to Chester without Armanda. Bringing her back was the one thing she really wanted to do. Still able to smell Armanda's perfume, Ellie knew Kent would have forgiven her, if she had succeeded in producing his own flesh and blood—even though it would be to say good-bye before she ever said hello. She knew giving their child away was wrong, and she had failed to vindicate her mistake.

Ellie hung her head pitifully as she handled the cordless phone wanting to call someone, but no one could help her get through this. As much as Manny loved her,

Ellie had to fight this battle all by herself—a daughter who stubbornly refused knowing her birth mother.

Cousin Mae's admonishing speech, about adopted children hating their birth parents, colored Ellie's thoughts as she propped up the stuffed animals to lay back. Ellie saw in a flash that she was like Armanda for not forgiving her mother for leaving her the night they had cried at the mercy of Mr. Spooky. The loneliness and emptiness she felt was nothing less than what Armanda was feeling. If she could not forgive her mother, Claudine, who had spent sixteen years with her, then how could she expect Armanda who had never known her to open up and erase the years of pain?

An ambulance rushed by blowing its siren on the street below the building. Ellie jumped at the noise, which startled her. To find some comfort, she reached for a stuffed animal poking her on the bed. Thinking about Armanda and her mother, she squeezed the stuffed orange and black striped tiger close to her chest. Although the room was not hot, she felt heat creeping over her body. Ellie was releasing her own feelings of abandonment, and she forgave her mother Claudine.

"Please forgive me, mother," Ellie spoke softly to herself.

Forgiving Claudine made Ellie question the way she had sidled up to Kent. She had thrown her feelings out of balance, trying to find the perfect time to tell him about Armanda. She had hoped if he loved her enough that it would have made her choice to give up Armanda forgivable. Now, her forgiveness of Claudine warmed

Ellie's spirit and opened her heart to releasing the years of grief for placing Armanda for adoption.

The key to her peace was not Kent's act of forgiving her but her very own self-forgiveness. Clutching tighter the stuffed animal, she sought forgiveness from within for having done the same thing to her child. She also had abandoned Armanda. Amazed at how tough the years had been, while carrying a torch of resentment for Claudine and regretting her choice of adoption, Ellie felt some peace.

Her trip was not what she had hoped, but very worthwhile. It gave Ellie her life back with peace. Tonight with the turn of events, Ellie accepted Claudine's choice to leave Chester, regardless of whether she had meant to abandon her and never come back. Claudine's choice was not for Ellie to second guess. She had to accept its reality and go on with her life. Starting tomorrow, she would tell Manny about her past and begin to mend the fences she had built between them.

She used her broken nail finger to dial her husband. Her hand moved automatically around the map of numbers. After one full ring, he answered.

"Hello Honey, I've finished doing what I can here. I'll see you on Sunday. I miss you." Ellie spoke into the tiny black mouthpiece as she fidgeted sitting in the center of the bed with her shoes on.

"How are you doing?" Manny asked. He was curious to know if Ellie had found her daughter.

"Today was eventful, I'll give you all the details when I get home. I'm sorry I had to leave you," she said.

Manny caught the "I" and knew that she was coming home alone. Too bad for Ellie, but he could hear the resolve in her voice.

"I'll be on time and waiting for you. We miss you here. Sonny has asked about you," Manny said.

"Oh, how's he holding up?" she asked, concerned that she had let him down.

Feeling sorry for the aging man, Ellie recognized her failure to bring Armanda home would hurt him the most. She began to untie her shoes, expecting her cousin to barge in any minute.

"Sonny seem like he's doing his best. I know the crowds are getting to him, but he's a trooper." Manny made it clear that he had seen Sonny.

"Thank goodness," Ellie responded, really too tired to talk on the telephone.

"Sonny mentioned what he wanted to talk about before the storm," he said and was interrupted by Ellie.

"What did he want?" she asked, deciding to take the opportunity to begin telling Manny some of what had been her secrets.

"We can talk about it later, but he's interested in me farming his land now that Kent is gone," Manny said, sounding like Kent had packed his bags and left for a trip.

"Oh, that's interesting," Ellie said, wondering how he could do such when they had planned on leaving Chester after the four years demanded by the will.

She heard Cousin Mae's heavy feet in the hallway.

"Ellie, you sound different," Manny said, collecting his thoughts about her and their life in Chester.

He wanted to share with Ellie that her mother had not abandoned her. He knew for a fact that Claudine's body was resting beside the man who paid the price of being alone after her death. After seeing the estate attorney, Manny knew, in near death, his grandfather had realized his shortcomings in life and assured through his will that he would finally rest in peace by one person he had loved.

"I have something to show you when you get back," Manny said, concluding it was best to wait.

He was not sure that Ellie could bear one more unexpected event. She needed time to deal with the disappointment of returning to Chester without her daughter.

After saying good-bye, Ellie held the telephone to her heart so relieved that Manny was her husband. She was lucky to have him. Ellie curled her body up in a neat and comfortable ball in the center of the bed and fell asleep, finally free.

Coming to Chicago to find her daughter had given Ellie the courage to see herself. She saw the root of her pain, which allowed her to resolve the hurt and forgive Claudine for leaving. Ellie was finally at peace with the secrets she had harbored since fleeing from Chester as a young woman.

The door squeaked and Cousin Mae rushed in asking, "You sleep in here?" being her usual self.

Ellie raised her head and said sleepily, "Yes."

"Honey, I don't want you going to bed mad at me. I never thought you would find out about the other terms of the adoption papers," she said, seeking an apology.

"It's alright, I'm fine," Ellie said, shaking her head to have her agree.

"I'm sorry. See, if we hadn't put that in the papers, the term to keep the baby's name Armanda would have gone out the door. And I knew it was the only thing you had for the child." She looked upset.

"I really am, OK." She reassured her cousin feeling some relief from her tangled emotions.

"Missy, I insisted on the name, and they literally twisted my arm to say that the parents were no longer living." Cousin Mae apologized.

"You're forgiven. Thanks for helping me today," Ellie said, raising up to speak. "I'm so tired. I need some rest," Ellie said as she yawned and pulled the covers over her.

"Going to bed this early, you must be pregnant," Cousin Mae sassed.

"Not likely," Ellie responded, ready for her cousin to call it a night. "Good night, I'll see you in the morning." She blurted from under the covers.

"What about Armanda? Should we make a plan for tomorrow, you've got another day." Cousin Mae kept talking.

"What else can we do? I can't make her. I can only hope. There is always hope." Ellie prayed. She was at peace for trying.

CHAPTER THIRTEEN

*E*arly Sunday morning, Ellie woke up still tired after a full day of not feeling so well but ready to go home. She smelled Cousin Mae's famous vegetable omelet as she came to the breakfast table fully packed, carrying her one bag, a backpack, and a smile. They were having the tasty omelet and homemade buttered biscuits on her last day in her old hometown.

"Well, you look like you're ready for home. I'm going to miss you, Ellie," Cousin Mae said. She stood over the stove flipping an omelet to one side. "Hold your plate for me." She gestured with a spatula in one hand. It slid easily, dripping a little grease.

With the smell closer to her nose, Ellie felt faint. She hurriedly put the plate down and ran to the bathroom.

"What's wrong?" Cousin Mae asked and followed Ellie. "You, OK in there?" she spoke through the door.

"Yes," Ellie managed. "I'll be out in a minute."

Cousin Mae walked back to the kitchen, saying under her breath, "She isn't nothing but pregnant."

Out of the bathroom, Ellie was fine.

"I heard you." She eyed Cousin Mae as she sat down at the table and feasted on a dry biscuit plus a piece of fruit.

Tracking down her adopted daughter made Chicago feel much different than when she left. Going through the good times with Cousin Mae in their last moments together, Ellie missed Manny and home.

Sitting relaxed and full in front of empty plates, Cousin Mae looked at Ellie and said sadly, "All finished, I guess you're ready?"

She wished Ellie could stay a little longer.

"We just as well get moving to the airport. We're making good time on our schedule." Ellie checked her watch, seeing the frown on her cousin's face. "You can come to the farm anytime you want to. It's not as bad as you think." She smiled. "Do you promise?"

"It's a deal," Cousin Mae said, like they were partners in crime.

Thirty minutes later, the faithful old stationwagon pulled lop-sided up to the curbside check-in area. They gave each other the biggest hugs, and Ellie stepped out of the car a more complete woman than when she was picked up. Wearing black knit pants, a soft pink cotton shirt with a Bolero jacket, Ellie had done her best to bring Armanda back for the funeral.

Out of curiosity, she asked a stranger for directions to the Lost and Found before checking for her departure gate. Ellie carried her bags the full distance to the opposite end near the baggage area to the Lost and Found desk. At the counter, Ellie leaned over its top to a redhead making doodles. She inquired whether Armanda had claimed the ticket that she had called into the airline.

"Madam, I'm sorry, but no one has claimed the ticket." A person behind the desk reported. "Do you want it back?"

Loud pages shouted continuously in the background, making it difficult for her to hear. But the head shaking and facial expression told Ellie no. Although, she saw little hope of returning with Armanda, Ellie decided to leave the ticket, hoping there was still some time.

"No, you hold it for Ms. Fairweather," she calmly stated and began to traverse the large airport to make her flight.

Thinking about Manny and getting home, she made her way through the busy airport to her gate. Ellie sat down beside a family with two children in the crowded boarding area. Her flight was overbooked.

The ticket attendant kept telling people like a broken record, "Sorry, it's full."

Ellie knew if Armanda did not show soon that she would be bumped from the flight, but Armanda was nowhere to be seen.

Ellie settled into her chair and held her bags, oblivious to the busy place. Tomorrow she had the funeral to attend. Her old lover, Kent, would be laid to rest. The thought of him being gone was still unbelievable. Ellie began reminiscing of the days they had played as children in the barn. Those days were truly bygones. She asked herself if she was being punished for her deceit of Kent. Ellie wanted to cry about her past actions, but that could not change anything.

While in a fog with her eyes closed, the boarding area had cleared and Ellie sat by herself. The loud final call for all passengers to board jarred Ellie's attention. Sitting alone, she looked around one more time hoping to see Armanda. The wide corridor was still busy with people going and coming, but Armanda was not coming.

Ellie waved her confirmed ticket at the attendant, and he hurried her through the gate. She stopped him.

"Help me please," she grasped at the last chance that Armanda was late. "Will you page someone who is supposed to catch this flight? Please, sir, please," Ellie begged.

Very upset, she rattled the information to him.

The young man stepped to the counter and lifted his microphone, "Paging Armanda Fairweather, will you please call extension number 1865 immediately." He repeated the page feeling sorry for Ellie.

"We can only wait a second for her," he said. Checking the time, he somberly added, "Madam, this flight is full anyway. There are no seats available."

He held out his hand for her ticket.

Ellie panicked, "I'll give her mine."

"Sorry, you must board now."

Ellie gave him her ticket and walked through the tunnel to the aircraft all by herself. Inside, she moved freely to her seat with the aisle clear, since everyone else had settled down. People had their magazines and newspapers up to their faces, getting comfortable for the flight. She shoved along bleak, looking for seat number

16A. It was a window seat. Moving toward her assigned row, Ellie could see that someone occupied the space next to hers. A person with their nose in a newspaper was sitting in the seat she had purchased for Armanda.

" Excuse me," Ellie said, annoyed and letdown.

The newspaper lowered, and there was Armanda. Ellie screamed. Everyone around her turned to see what was the matter as the airplane began to taxi for take-off.

"I'm sorry," she said to the passengers staring at her, including Armanda.

Armanda stood up to let her in while the flight attendant began going through the emergency procedures, and Ellie kept quiet. The air between them was thick. Ellie took her seat, knowing it was best to only speak but say no more. Armanda was on the flight, just like she had hoped.

Armanda's heart skipped beats as she sat not knowing how to relate to Ellie. On Friday, after Ellie had banged on the wall and yelled her final plea through the door, Armanda had cried. She had stood by the door unable to register that her real mother had found her. What had just happened and why greatly confused her. It was way too much to process as she camped in her apartment the next day afraid of how she was feeling.

She had wondered for years what her real mother and father had been like. She had longed to know her people. The questions had played on her mind, since her parents shared that she was adopted and her birth parents were dead.

At age ten, Armanda accepted her life would never change being in the prominent Chicagoian family. Her life was privileged and planned from Catholic schools to college. She was on break from Northwestern University, deciding whether to take an internship to complete her master degree or spend a year abroad.

Fighting the urges of her adopted mother to not make this trip, Armanda hid behind the newspaper in awe of the circumstances that could change her life. She was distressed that years had passed with the false information. Armanda loved the only mother she ever knew. Seeing her cry with disapproval, after Armanda decided to make this trip, had caused much added unrest to the unusual situation. Now, she was flying to a funeral for her natural father, having little time to make sense of what to do. Armanda rode the complete flight beside Ellie without talking.

Four hours later and one airplane change, they touched down in Albany where Manny would be waiting. Ellie was close to being home with her daughter and a blessing to Sonny. Still not speaking, Armanda made her way to the terminal walking ten paces behind Ellie. Armanda carried her bag, looking confident as she strolled in a linen white blouse and black pants. Her fancy belt buckle and pearls gave a rich touch to her casual attire.

With a bouquet of fresh flowers, Manny stood next to the redcoat guy who greeted the connecting passengers, watching for Ellie.

"There you are," he said to his wife coming up the ramp and opened his arms for a hug. She charged into his arms and held onto his extra large shirt tucked into blue jeans.

When he opened his eyes, he saw the spitting image of Kent and Ellie in the beautiful young woman standing behind her. He was expecting only Ellie from their conversations on Friday and Saturday night. After her return from Chicago, Manny was hoping Ellie would clear all the secrets and half-truths between them. It had been too much for too long. He wondered if she had deliberately said nothing. He wanted to snatch the letter out of his pocket and give it to her, so Ellie could just come clean. Manny was striving to understand Ellie, but she just kept on heaping more for him to deal with.

Stepping out of their embrace, Ellie said, "Manny, this is Armanda." She was too afraid to use the word "daughter."

"It's nice to meet you." They shook hands as he looked askance at Ellie.

Ellie moved closer to him and quietly whispered, "Honey, we'll talk later at home, but she's mine and Kent's daughter. She's here for the funeral." Ellie put her hand firmly on Manny's arm, hoping he would say nothing. She rushed to add, "I know you're shocked, but the situation is very tender, just bear with me until we're alone, please."

Manny took Ellie's cue and grabbed the bags after being introduced. It was apparent that Armanda was not staying long. She had one very light, small carry-on.

"Thank you," she said to him when he lifted her bag.

While going to the car with Armanda a good distance behind them, Ellie made it clear to Manny that she had not known if Armanda was coming to Chester until she sat down on the airplane.

"Remember the other night when I said things had been eventful for the day; we found Armanda that day. But she was adamant that she would not be coming to Chester, even for one day. So I accepted her words and made peace with her decision. I'd tried my best to convince her." Ellie was longwinded. She wenched at the unexpected words coming from her mouth. But she kept talking unsure of what Manny was thinking, "I'm sorry you're surprise, but I'm surprised too." She blinked her eyes trying to look steady at him. Manny would not say a word, so she continued, "She will not speak to me. She didn't talk to me the whole trip." Ellie shook her head, wondering what it would take for Armanda to make peace with her. She momentarily stopped near the car and whispered, "Manny, she's having a time with all this. So please bear with me." Ellie pleaded some more with her husband to understand.

"Honey, we can talk later. There's something that I have to show you," he spoke not wanting Armanda to overhear them as they stood at the car.

"I have something to tell you also," Ellie said, thinking that she was pregnant.

In the parking lot, Manny loaded the bags and headed to Chester. Ellie sat quietly as Manny and Armanda talked sporadically about living in Chicago.

✳✳✳

On the road to Chester, Armanda viewed a world of rolling fields and greenery. There was not much to see but wide open space, a patchwork of land broken by miniature fences. This was as far South as she ever had been. In front of them, tractors pulled doubled trailers piled high with shelled corn. Yellow dust sprinkled their ride until Manny safely passed it on the two-lane road. Bows of white cotton hanging on brown stalks were the first she had seen. Large lovebugs, stuck in twos, bounced off the car's window shield. Armanda saw styles of houses she had only read about. The rain washed row houses raised her curiosity about her people living in the South as she brushed her bangs out of her eyes.

At home in Chester, Manny and Ellie settled Armanda into a guestroom and said, "Welcome to our house. You can stay as long as you wish."

The sun was shining brightly in the all green room where the three stood feeling awkward. Ellie had intentionally decorated this one with a femine touch and the bedroom across the hall in more masculine hues of brown. Once Manny put her bags down, Armanda opted to take a nap. Then he led Ellie out of the room.

"I need to show you something," he said, ready to head to the grave of her mother under a tree at the north border.

"Honey, I'm almost too tired to move after the long trip. Can it wait?" Ellie suggested too drained of energy to keep going. But she saw in his eyes that it was important to him. "Sure," Ellie gave Manny all of her attention.

He held her flowers, admiring his wife's beauty.

"Where are we going?" she asked curiously.

"For a walk," Manny stated, looking for a vase.

"Let me get a glass of water and give me five minutes to change clothes," she said, trying to revive herself to please her husband.

Ellie knew that it was as good a time as anytime to divulge all the issues that she had contended with before fleeing and since moving back to Chester. She disappeared upstairs while Manny handled the flowers. In minutes, Ellie came downstairs wearing jeans and an oversize thin summer sweater. Manny began their walk to the border. He wanted Ellie to know the truth.

In the front yard, she saw her gardening getting better after the heavy rain of last week. Holding her hand, Manny led the way toward the abandoned barn. They chatted about her trip, and Ellie spilled her secrets: she and Kent were about to be married when she left for Chicago, not knowing that she was pregnant with his child.

Manny listened.

They neared the north border, and Ellie saw a short patch of trees cleared at the edge of the thicket before the grassy field. She gasped at the disturbance that Manny had started but called off, once he found the graves. Just a few trees were gone, and the barn was still hidden.

"What happened here?" she asked and stopped walking when she realized where they were going.

"Why are we going this way?" Ellie pointed at the border.

"Trust me Ellie, you need to see this," Manny said, continuing to lead the way on a path that she had traveled many times to meet Kent.

Moving on, Manny came clean with his intention to clear the border for pulpwood and hay, until he found something that he had to show her.

Ellie was sure it was the letter. So she begin to tell him everything before they reached the huge tree. Her Sunday meetings had been in the old barn, sitting with the wide windowless spaces like eyes staring at them. Behind it and under the farthest tree, Ellie saw the grave in the clearing.

"This is what I want you to see," Manny said, as she walked closer.

Ellie stooped down at the belted marker. She was shocked when she read the name "Claudine" whittled into the cross. Without speaking, she put her hands on it and touched the necklace. She remembered it so well. It was her mother's favorite piece of jewelry. Ellie cried. Tears rolled from the inside corners of her eyes. She wept freely and got closer as if to touch her mother. Ellie knelt on the dirt and read the dates.

Etched in the cross were her mother's birthday and oddly no date of death, but a date was beside the word "found." Ellie pondered and then realized like Manny had that her mother probably died the night of her disappearance. She cried tears of sadness that her mother was dead. And Ellie cried tears of joy that Claudine was resting in peace from all the pain she had endured at the hands of Mr. Spooky.

Silent for a few minutes as Manny stood with his hand on her shoulder, Ellie put the pieces together like a puzzle. The massive root of the tree where her mother was buried triggered Ellie. She figured Claudine must have lost her life trying to reach the abandoned barn in the dark. Feeling the relief of knowing at last what had happened to her mother, she accepted that Claudine had died after stumbling over the root and hurting herself.

Ellie showered in the truth that her mother had never abandoned her. She had already forgiven Claudine in her heart for leaving. Ellie settled her differences with her long lost mother the day she located Armanda. It did not matter if Claudine had left her and never intended to come back. Now, she loved Claudine even more for being the mother who would have saved them both, if only she had lived. Ellie was relieved.

"Manny, this is my mother's grave," Ellie said, feeling his presence. "She left me with her awful, common-law husband, Mr. Spooky."

Ellie caught Manny's eyes after she said the mean man's name, and she turned away from Manny.

"He was your grandfather," Ellie said unwillingly and afraid to feel for the old man even though her husband was so very different from his grandfather.

"Ellie, I know now that your Mr. Spooky was my grandfather." He reached down to help Ellie up from the ground.

"You knew all along?" she abruptly questioned him.

"No, honey, but look."

Manny pointed out his grandfather's unmarked grave next to her mother's.

"This told me. They're here side by side." He gestured at the raised ground. "Ellie, he carved her grave marker with his hand. It's his writing. I can tell by the long narrow letters he used in the field notes he left me."

Bitter about the past, Ellie refused to acknowledge that Mr. Spooky had ever loved her mother or scrawled the epitaph "Rest in Peace, My Love." She dared not to think for one moment that he had been gracious enough to bury her.

"No, this can't be," she said, resisting the truth.

"In his will he wanted his grave unmarked and undisclosed. This has to be it," Manny concluded.

"No," Ellie shook her head.

"I was equally amazed, and while you were gone, I saw the attorney who handled the estate. He didn't deny it, Ellie. Although, he wouldn't break his client-attorney oath and say 'yes' outright." Manny explained and understood why Ellie had been distant. "This is it, I can feel it."

"Manny," Ellie said, unable to complete her thought.

"Ellie, he loved her in his own way," Manny offered of his grandfather, wanting her to forgive and let go her ill feelings.

"Manny, coming back to Chester had its faults, but coming to the very place I had lived was devastating to me." Ellie spoke to the graves.

"Sweetheart, there's no doubt you've been through a lot since returning here," he said as she dropped his hand.

Their fingers were entangled, but she made an effort to free hers.

"All his contempt, his cruelness," she repeated out loud to herself while standing at the foot of Mr. Spooky's grave. "I couldn't help myself some days, Manny, and it was hard to love you knowing who he was to you." Ellie ruffled through her words in tears.

"It's been tough on both of us."

"I know that I hurt you. I'm so very sorry," she sobbed. "Please forgive me. You're nothing like him." Ellie held out her hand for Manny.

He reached for hers.

"I'm happy knowing you love me and that my mother has found peace," Ellie said still crying and hoping that Armanda could forgive her.

She clutched Manny as if she was desperately holding on to life.

"Hey, it's going to be fine," he said, sensing that something else bothered Ellie. "What's wrong?"

He rubbed her back to comfort her.

"It's Armanda. She'll never understand this like you have. I made some big mistakes, and I'm willing to admit my actions were wrong. I just hope Armanda can forgive me." Ellie confessed to Manny her true feelings. "She's my daughter, my only child," Ellie whispered, remembering her morning sickness.

She began to tell him of her pregnancy signs, but Manny took a step back and pulled the note from his pocket.

Ellie was stunned to see Manny with her letter that she had left for Kent. Ellie's heart sank, seeing the flap was opened.

She was embarrassed.

"Maybe this will help Armanda to understand. It did for me." Manny offered the letter to her.

He had read it many times during Ellie's absence.

She slowly reached for it.

In spite of her letter to Kent revealing all her secrets, Manny still supported and loved Ellie. He had known her secrets for over a week. He was disappointed in her secrecy, but he understood. Ellie had expected Manny would have been angry to discover her faults.

Ellie took the letter without questioning her husband. She assumed it was lost in the storm, and he had found it when he located the graves while clearing the north border. Silently, they started their walk back home, hand in hand.

"I have something to tell you."

Ellie leaned into him relieved that she had shared her secrets with Manny, and the truth was out.

They looked into each other's eyes. "I think we're having a baby," she said happily.

Manny stopped and shouted his surprise, "A baby!" He lifted Ellie from her feet, saying "Yes, yes!" He was thrilled and swirled her around twice. Her legs topped the tall grass.

Ellie looked back at her mother's grave, accepting more that it was her destiny to be next to Mr. Spooky. She and Manny walked in the tall brush under a painted purple sky. The sun glowed behind the perimeter of the pine trees as Manny walked with Ellie—the wife he wanted beside him. He was fortunate that he had decided against disturbing their kin's resting place. Now, it would forever be their hideaway.

✳✳✳

When Ellie and Manny returned from walking at the north border, it was too late for Armanda to meet Sonny.

She had stayed in the guestroom, refusing to come out and eat supper. The next morning, she was dressed in black with her bags packed ready to go to the funeral when she came out.

The whole trip, she had offered Ellie nothing more than kind "hellos" in response to Ellie's greetings. At breakfast, she talked mostly with Manny about going to his alma mater, Northwestern University. They went through all the popular places in Chicago, including Manny's favorite old comedy spot, All Jokes Aside. Ellie wanted in on the conversation, but her senses could feel the tension in Armanda. She was clearly here for Kent's funeral, not Ellie.

Before getting into the Volvo, Armanda asked Manny to place her bags in the trunk, because she wanted to go directly from the funeral to the airport for a flight back to Chicago. Armanda was only staying for the one day that Ellie had requested.

Hearing her statement, Ellie held onto the letter too afraid to give it to Armanda like she had planned to do. Armanda was not ready to understand or forgive. She was quiet on the way to meet Sonny.

A processional of cars had lined up at the funeral home with Sonny in the lead vehicle behind the hearse. As Manny drove up, a police car was leading the way out of the parking lot. With their lights on, the vehicles paraded to New Salem Missionary Baptist Church for Kent's funeral. Manny and Ellie had hoped to have Armanda ride in the Lincoln Town Car with Sonny, but they missed it.

In the churchyard, Manny quickly parked, and Ellie ushered Armanda up to the front of the processional line. She gave Sonny a hug, and in their embrace, she gently told Sonny Armanda was Kent's daughter. Ellie stood back, squeezed his arm for reassurance, and placed their hands together.

Still holding hands, Sonny and Armanda saw the funeral director nod at the pallbearers to proceed down the aisle. Ellie and Manny followed behind them as the choir sang "I'll Fly Away." The sisters of the church belted the tune, fanning fast on the hot day. As the church crowded to near standing room only, they moaned the words in perfect harmony. Some rocked from side to side, and others lifted their hands to the sky.

With everyone seated, the minister opened the service asking for God's blessings. Sonny sat numb beside Armanda on the front row. Ellie and Manny was across the aisle on the opposite front pew. During the eulogy, Sprewell Jr. slid into the back row with his papers in his jacket breast pocket. As a chill of grief came over the crowded church, he patted his chest securing the deed that would transfer every acre of Sonny's land to him. Today he meant to have Sonny's signature and finally the rights to the Vinson's land.

People were curious about the young woman, escorting Sonny into the church. Heads turned and lips smacked as whispers among the congregation flowed from pew to pew. Members wondered in hushed voices who the young woman might be.

Armanda stared at the opened casket in front of her. Her long-lashed eyes were fixed on her deceased father.

Tears swelled from the outside corners of her eyes and pushed through the wall that she had built up to protect herself while visiting Chester. Overcome with sorrow, she felt a connection with being here.

Sonny put his arms around her and tried to comfort his granddaughter who whimpered. She was indeed the spitting image of Kent and Ellie. He studied her profile as he sat comforting her. On the day of Kent's death, Ellie had bent her head into his passenger window and promised him everything was going to be all right. Although she told him that Kent had a child, Sonny had been dazed. Ellie promised him that she would find Armanda and bring her back for the funeral, but he thought it was strange that she had only mumbled after she exited his car the day Kent died. Sonny was clueless as to what Ellie had said. But he could not deny that he felt better having Armanda by his side. He knew Kent was smiling from above.

The noise about the young woman who sat beside Sonny on the front row made its way to Sprewell Jr. He choked at hearing what fluttered about the congregation—that the lovely young woman was somehow Kent's daughter. He coughed into his hand, shaking his head. He absolutely would not, on his daddy's grave, accept it. The first opportunity to come his way, he was determined that Sonny would sign the deed, no matter the nonsense the gossips were spreading.

The recessional began when the choir broke into humming "Amazing Grace." The pallbearers simultaneously lifted the casket onto their shoulders. They stooped low in unison and then stood tall. One grunted.

Strolling behind the body, Sonny and Armanda passed through the center aisle, leading a line of tows. At the back of the sanctuary Sprewell Jr.'s eyes locked on them. He batted, seeing the undeniable and deep resemblance of her to the Vinsons. Sprewell Jr. immediately got up and stormed out the church ahead of everyone, almost knocking Sonny down. Sonny's heart skipped beats, knowing what Sprewell Jr. had expected after the funeral. He marched on with his head high, intending to ignore him since he had an heir for his land. Although Kent was gone, his land was safe for the next generation. He held tightly to Armanda moving to the graveyard.

At the gravesite, Kent's body was lowered into the ground as the minister mashed a red rose over the casket.

"Ashes to ashes and dust to dust," he spoke the final words, and dismissed the mourners that stirred like young soldiers granted permission to be at ease.

After hearing those words, Ellie felt Kent's soul touch her heart. It was good-bye and thank you from her friend and old lover. Kent's death was the guiding force that brought her secret about Armanda to light. Ellie was finally at peace with Kent and all her secrets. His dying helped her with what no one else alive could. It was destiny for her to reunite with their daughter.

Everyone mumbled and fumbled their way through the cemetery to their cars, leaving Sonny and Armanda sitting all alone. Ellie stood by the Lincoln parked on the church ground that waited to motor Sonny back home. Sitting in the sunshine, he talked to Armanda about Kent, giving her story after story about her father. They began to bond through memories of a dead father and son.

Many hours passed with the two together in front of the grave covered with dirt. They missed entirely the fellowship gathering in the church's basement. The funeral director had completed his work and taken his gear, leaving them sitting among the many flower arrangements and plants.

Before the sun settled on the horizon, they rose from the red velvet cloaked sitting chairs and descended to the last vehicle waiting, Manny's and Ellie's Volvo. A few steps away from his son's grave, Sonny turned back and picked the prettiest blooming plant to give to Armanda. Holding it in one arm, she and Sonny leaned on each other.

Walking to the car, her cares were with Sonny as strands of hair escaped her bun and fell from the heat. Her simple but elegant long flowing black dress touched the grass as she bent, helping him to the car. She ignored the rocks and pebbles that notched her soft leather pumps.

With their spirits revived after the celebration of life, Manny drove them all home. Pulling into the Vinson's yard beside the leaning mailbox, Sonny's aging body slowly clamored out of the backseat. Armanda quickly opened her door and circled the car to assist him. She patiently walked him to the front door. She came back and asked for her bag.

"Thanks for your help," she said to Manny who took her bag from the trunk.

"If you need anything, just let us know," he said and reentered the car. "You just call us, now, when you want to leave for the airport."

Moved by Armanda's devotion to Sonny, Ellie could only hope that Armanda would choose to stay long enough to get to know the both of them. She was delighted that her daughter was not rushing back to Chicago.

Armanda lifted the light bag with her few belongings in it. She waved to both of them, but more directly at Manny than Ellie.

CHAPTER FOURTEEN

*T*hree days later, Armanda was still in Chester and adored her grandfather, Sonny. Getting updated on her family past, she wiggled her legs as she lay across her father's bed, during Sonny's show-and-tell, including a few more World War II stories. She laughed at the funny ones and shed tears to the sad stories. She found him charming. She was enjoying their time together, getting to know him and learning about her father. Every picture in the house, including Sonny's favorites on his nightstand, was shown to her.

The day after the funeral, she had picked through the piles of photo books. Armanda wanted all the details of who was in each picture, when it was taken and what happened on the day it was shot. Once she began relaxing, Sonny shared with Armanda what had happened to her father. He explained that Kent was shot in an unfortunate accident by a rookie police officer. A long way from healing, Sonny told her the details of the unforgettable day. He had blamed no one for his son's death. He only said that it was God's will for him. He became emotional remembering what a good son Kent was, and how he was no problem at all to him. There were moments that he spoke as if Kent was in the next room. When Sonny did, he would stop and catch his bearings as Armanda respected his feelings. Her simple presence was comforting.

On the porch, they had sat silently rocking, enjoying the sounds of the world. Before the day was over they played bingo to have something to do. Sonny wanted her comfortable in his home, and later that evening, he took her to town, insisting she purchase whatever she needed to stay as long as she wanted to.

On her second day after getting used to being in the house full of men's stuff, Armanda had scrounged around doing some of her father's chores. It was cheerier with her touch. She opened the heavy curtains to let the sunshine in. She cleaned the kitchen and polished all the furniture as she busied herself while dealing with knowing her parents had been alive. Armanda was not sure if she should let herself go with what was happening.

She had longed for the feeling of a close family. Her heritage was in Chester and the 400-acre farm that had been in the Vinson family for three generations, waiting for the fourth. Sonny had mentioned that she was his only heir and would inherit his land. With Kent gone, they discussed what to do with the farm and who would manage the daily details. Armanda had some decisions to make.

During their many conversations, Sonny explained the Moccasin Pond deal to her. He had started like he did with Kent, "It was 1944..." As Sonny told her, he was reliving the fear of just how close the deal came to taking his land.

Armanda sat with her hand on her chin listening intently at the sad past. She frowned at the tension of the crowd that had surrounded him and threatened his life at Moccasin Pond. She took a deep breath impressed with the honorable man that her great grandfather was to stick with the deal. When Sonny finished, she was floored by the history of her past generation endurance in the South. Armanda held Sonny's hand until she thought he was comfortable, after he had passionately bore to her the ill chapters of his life on the land.

On the third day, Sonny shared with Armanda Stella's dreams to move North. She learned about her Grandmother's pregnancy with her Uncle James. He showed her James' navy suit, before they made breakfast. She continued to ask many questions about her family as they sat at the breakfast table eating oatmeal and toast. In the middle of another World War II story, the telephone rang making Sonny catch his breath.

"I'll get it," Armanda said to him. She reached for the phone on the kitchen counter and answered, "Hello."

It was Ellie.

"Armanda, I would like to see you," Ellie said, hoping her daughter would say yes.

She knew it would not be long before Armanda decided to leave for Chicago, and she wanted to know her daughter as a young woman. Their marred past could not change, but their future could be different.

"I'm going into town today to take care of some business for my grandfather," Armanda said properly without realizing she had used words for the first time that acknowledged she was part of the Vinson family. "I'm sorry not today," she spoke quickly to Ellie.

"It won't take long," Ellie said, holding the letter in her hand.

"Maybe some other time but not today," she responded curtly, "Good-bye."

Armanda hung up the telephone and left her hand on the receiver in a daze.

"You really should consider seeing Ellie," Sonny said, overhearing her conversation. "She loved your father dearly. She always has been like family to us," he offered, hoping to encourage Armanda to see her birth mother.

Armanda squirmed feeling delicate in the situation. She adjusted her cotton blouse and the bow on her skirt. Her eyes floated about the house as she wondered what to do. The coffeepot needed turning off, so she did it. She was very uncomfortable with the thought of dealing with Ellie.

"I'm off to town in a minute. You need me to do anything else for you?" Armanda asked, ready to recap their earlier plans.

"No, you can handle it. Let me give you directions to town." Sonny repeated them again just to hear himself talk. He spilled the easy left, then right and left.

Her long skirt trailed the floor as she stood up to clear the table. Since the funeral, she had left her face clear of makeup and had enjoyed the freedom of being natural. The past few days of visiting with Sonny she had liked being outside in the country air, sitting on the porch in a rocking chair reading her dad's books. It was much different than her highrise apartment in Chicago. She enjoyed the nature walks, the birds chirping, and wild sunflowers littering the fence rows. Being in Chester was more than what she had expected, but she needed to face Ellie. She was hurt knowing her own flesh and blood gave her away, after believing for so long there was no one.

"I'm gone," Armanda yelled before she shut the screen door.

"OK, precious child. You be careful," Sonny said and walked to the door to see his granddaughter out.

Inside by himself, he went straight to his room. He opened his foot chest and rummaged through his important papers to find the deed to his property. Sprewell Jr. would not catch him short again, and Sonny planned to have the deed transferred to Armanda as soon as possible. In a box at the bottom of the chest that Stella used many years ago, he ruffled through more old tarnished documents and found his deed. Holding the deed to his land, Sonny pined for his sons while prizing his grandchild who had saved the land.

Armanda impressed him with her knowledge of growing flowers and her love for history. She had asked questions about people and things that he had long forgotten about. He enjoyed talking and telling his war stories to a willing listener.

Armanda drove the truck along the route Sonny had described. His directions were hardly needed to make it to the small town. After hearing how her dad had the major responsibility of running the farm, she was determined to find someone to take his place.

Yesterday, she had talked with Sonny and some of his farm workers. Today, she wanted to check out a lead that one had given her on Zachary Glasser. Armanda had heard that he could get the job done.

She parked the truck in front of the cafe, hoping to find him. Inside, Tall Nancy seated Armanda and licked her chops at the fresh ears she would bend, gossiping.

"Honey, right here will do you fine," she said as she placed Armanda in a booth all by herself. "What can I get you?"

"Nothing but coffee. I'm looking for someone by the name of Zachary Glasser. Is he here?" Armanda asked.

"Sure, that's him sitting at the counter on the third stool." Tall Nancy pointed at Zachary waiting for noon to visit his mother. She smacked her chewing gum. "What do you want with him?" The question fell quickly from her tongue. "He killed your daddy," she said in one breath with plenty of drama in her voice.

"Excuse me," Armanda said unaware that Zachary was the police officer who had fired the fatal shot.

No one had told her who did. Even when she spoke in depth with Sonny about Zachary's farming skills, he never said a word against him. She was surprised to hear that the officer was Zachary. Feeling awkward, Armanda wanted some time to think, but Tall Nancy was calling him to the booth.

"Hey, Zachary, this pretty little gal wants to see you. Hurry up and get over her," she barked like she did to the kitchen help.

Zachary would pass time in the cafe each morning before making his visit to the nursing home to see his mother. He was desperately trying to keep control of himself and not let what had happened that deadly day wear his nerves. This morning, he dragged himself from the two rooms he had patched in Ma Resta's old sunken-in house. He made a fair offer to pay rent, but his prior boss who owned the place had refused one penny from him. He needed work because his last bit of money went to pay the nursing home bills for his mother's care. Zachary was unconcerned about his living conditions as long as his mother could get well.

He saw the young woman Tall Nancy was standing over pouring a cup of coffee and immediately recognized who she was. His palms sweated, and he grew timid about going over to the booth to meet her. Seeing her watching him walk across the cafe broke his heart and brought back the chain of events on the day of the shooting. It was haunting him.

A bit unsteady that Kent's daughter was looking for him, Zachary introduced himself and sat in the booth facing her. He shook her hand, looking off to the side. In spite of everything that had occurred lately in his life surrounding the loss of their farm, Zachary was bothered by the pain that he had caused the Vinsons.

"How you doing?" he asked, sitting uncomfortably in his seat.

"I'm fine," she managed, not sure how to handle the young man or Sonny's business at this point.

He had left the hiring decision to her.

Zachary looked down at the table. He had a kind spirit, and part of her felt sorry for him. Armanda decided he deserved a chance. She understood from her source that he needed the work to keep his mother in the nursing home. According to Sonny, his part at the scene of her father's death was unfortunate, and she would not hold it against him.

"I want to speak with you about working the Vinson farm. We need someone experienced to manage it since..." Armanda stopped before she referred to the incident. She saw the pain in his eyes as she was speaking. "Well, my grandfather is too old to work now. He has been retired for years. We could use your help." Armanda delivered her offer with much grace.

"Do you know who I am?" Zachary asked, having listened to his own inner voices without looking up.

His eyes focused on the table.

"I've heard nothing but good things about you," she said, unwilling to play into his self-pity.

"You know that I'm the one..." he stuttered, "...the one who shot your father." Zachary looked up for a second to check her reaction.

She raised her hand to stop him from falling deeper into despair.

"I heard it was an accident. I don't blame you," Armanda said, proud of herself for not holding it against him like she initially thought she would.

"If you're sure you want me to, I can start right away," he said, relieved.

"Come tomorrow. You take care of yourself," she said and put a dollar on the table for her coffee.

Satisfied, she shook on the deal, thinking Sonny would approve of the arrangement, since he knew about Zachary. It was his comments at the breakfast table that made her decide that Zachary fit the job.

He was moved by her compassion.

✳✳✳

On the way back to Sonny's, Armanda stopped unexpectedly by Ellie's house. She easily found her way to the large brick home where Ellie was rocking on the porch. She had morning sickness and came out earlier for some fresh air. Seeing Armanda drive up in the truck that she last saw Kent in, surprised Ellie, and she leaped to her feet.

"Get out and come in," she said.

Armanda exited the truck and walked along the colorful freshly planted annuals that hugged the hedges.

"This is good-bye. I'm leaving tomorrow and wanted you to know." She walked to the porch, stopping at the steps while talking. When she finished the last word Armanda looked down at the cat sunning on the glossy white steps.

"Oh," Ellie said, realizing that she would have no time with her. She had desired Armanda to understand why she was adopted. "Manny and I will be happy to take you to the airport," Ellie said, hoping that she could be with Armanda.

"That's not necessary, tell Manny good-bye for me." Armanda wheeled around to make her tracks to the truck.

"Wait," Ellie yelled, disturbing the cat that got up and ran frantically from the porch.

Armanda turned around.

"So soon," Ellie said, coming from the porch. Showing her disappointment that they had not bonded, she said maturely, "We'll miss you. I know Sonny is pleased that you came."

They both were silent, not knowing what else to say. Then Ellie reached for her daughter.

"May I have a hug?" she asked, knowing that she might never see her again.

Armanda hesitated.

Ellie felt sick in the bottom of her stomach, seeing the pain in Armanda's face. Armanda held her arms out and slowly embraced Ellie. Ellie touched her daughter for the first time since the two hours before her adoption. Hugging her birth mother, she was overcome with emotions. Scared of what she was feeling, Armanda tore away quickly from Ellie, still hurting. She started for the truck, but Ellie gently held her arm with one hand and reached into her Bermuda shorts pocket with the other. Ellie brought out the note that she had written to Kent.

"Here, this is for you. I wrote it to Kent," Ellie said, with tears streaming down her cheeks. "He would want you to read it. I want you to read it." She gave the note to Armanda who was leaving.

She took it and whipped around in the flowing skirt back to the truck. Ellie watched her daughter ride out of her life. She stood until the last sight of her was possible, hoping Armanda would look back. She never did.

***

The next day, Zachary reported promptly to work. His first duty was to take Sonny and Armanda to the airport for her departure on a noon flight. It was hard saying good-bye, but Armanda had done what she came to do. She had attended the funeral of her birth father and had gotten to know him through Sonny. Armanda counted it extra that she eased Sonny's worries about the land by hiring Zachary to manage the farm's daily operations.

Zachary smiled as he proudly assisted them. He felt forgiven by the mere fact that Sonny saw him as Sonny always had and not as the one who had killed his son. He owed a lot to this family for giving him the chance to place the incident behind him and move on with his life. Zachary was too young to have such heavy burdens.

On the road to the airport, he and Armanda teased about living in the South as she sat between him and Sonny in the truck, holding her plant. Sonny watched the farmlands out of his window. He was studying the best way to pass the deed of his property to Armanda. Would she take it? Would she ever call Chester home?

At the airport, Zachary hoisted Armanda's bag and paced himself with Sonny who was barely moving along. It was time to say farewell to her. After the changes in his life in the last year, Sonny would not dare suggest that she stay. Chester was new to her. He was grateful that she was found. His days of holding his family to the land were over. Sonny had suffered the short lives of all those he loved, and he still blamed it partly on the promise to keep the land. Armanda's existence was enough to keep solid on his promise, so he was just satisfied with her being family. Although, Armanda had made herself at home in his house, she had another life and was entitled to make her choice. Sonny would not wrestle with her as he had with James or deny her as he had Stella.

At the gate for departure, Armanda put her plant down, and she hugged Sonny. They held each other rocking from side to side. It was sobering to leave him, but her life was in Chicago.

"You're always welcome. You can come anytime. The land is yours," Sonny said, holding on to his only grandchild and heir.

Without worrying what her response would be, he presented the deed to Armanda, feeling no despair for all his toilsome labor under the sun. Losing the land to the Sprewells would have been a great misfortune.

"I want you to have it. It belongs to you," Sonny said, holding the deed out for her to take.

"I feel...," Armanda said with tears in her eyes.

"A lot has happened in the last year, and the best thing was finding you." Sonny took Armanda's hand and placed the deed in it. "Say 'yes' and make all the Vinsons happy, including your daddy," he said, sincerely.

Armanda accepted it graciously. In her heart, it was wrong to quibble with him. "Thank you. I love you," Armanda mouthed, trying to contain her emotions.

She was very taken by his trust in her. It was a gift that she had not expected. Armanda reached for her bags and the blooming plant from Zachary, and she walked backwards slowly away from her newfound kin. She would not forget Sonny. Armanda waved before disappearing in the tunnel to the aircraft. She anxiously came back to see his face, framing a memory of her endearing grandfather and waved one more time.

After boarding, she found her seat with tears flowing down her cheeks. Armanda closed her eyes to make sure she would remember Sonny's face.

Once the plane was in the air, she pulled out Ellie's note and carefully read it. In the first paragraph, she learned that her father never knew that she was born. After imagining what life would have been like if she had known him, Armanda was glad she had made the trip. She was overly grateful that she had shared his last moments on earth. His face was etched in her memory, and she pictured him sleeping like she first saw him.

After reading the note twice, Armanda understood more about her birth mother, Ellie, and her struggles. Hiding the fact of her existence, she had endured much pain after giving her up for adoption. The two hours Ellie had played with her, described in the letter, moved Armanda. The fears and secrets of Ellie's past enlightened her.

Feeling wonderful about having made the trip, Armanda realized that she was incomplete. There was mending to do, or she would fall into the same steps as her natural mother. Ellie had allowed mistakes to consume her life and lost people she cared about. Ellie's note written to Kent touched Armanda's heart deeply, and she wanted her mother just like any other little girl. Flying higher into the sunshine, Armanda looked down at the wide expanse of farmland below her, knowing she would return someday.

In Memory of sons shining in our hearts

Kenneth Bernard Jackson
7/20/58 – 9/15/99

James Edward Barney
1/11/61 – 12/17/95

Acknowledgements

Our Lord and Savior Jesus Christ without whom I can do nothing, He is so good and I thank Him; Thanks to so many wonderful people who have blessed me on my journey especially the following: to my parents Mr. and Mrs. Charlie O. Bush Sr. for their patience and belief in me as someone who can do anything; to my sisters Joyce Arline and Jacquelyn Drummer for numerous worthy comments, guidance and encouragement while writing the book; to my brothers and their families who inspire me to hold it together; to Connie Green who had more faith in me than I and edited until her fingers fell off; to Kimberlee Scott and Jeff Putnam for your expertise in writing; to Teresa Artis, Kathryn Flowers, Pat Laster, Debbie Combs, Bridgette Glover, Kay Hall, Arlene Gardaya, Arne B. Davis and Karen Davis for being the best cheerleaders and my biggest fans; to Vernesa Terrell one of my best friends who reminded me of my passion and who promised to buy ten books to get me to do what I love; to Herbert Edwards for believing in my mission; to the Wayne Glover and Joseph Roseborough families for making me a part of their clans; to Shawn Adkins a truly great person with a big heart; Wanda Pierson and the Jefferson Park Neighborhood Association; to those who first purchased a book when it was still in the its infancy stages at the Southern Sustainable Agriculture Working Group, Betty T. Bailey, William Reid, Daisy G. Campbell and Ben F. Burkett, and Frederick Watson of the Virginia Male Adolescent Network, Inc.; to my first Purchasers at the Federation of Southern Cooperatives Land Assistance Fund, Ronald Thornton, Leon Crump, and Joe C. Colvin of Colvin's Insurance Agency in Montgomery Alabama and to all the faithful lovers of the land there especially Monica Armster, Ralph Paige, Jerry Pennick, Cornelius Key, Deborah A. Johnson, Alice Paris, Heather Gray and Cornelius Blanding; to a very warm Professor Mark Latimore, Jr. at Fort Valley State University and Mark Thomas; to Professor Abdullah F.H. Muhammand at Alcorn State University; Susan R. Jones for her great suggestions; to Prince Brown, Director of Alumni Affairs Albany State University for your vote of confidence and interest; to Stinson A. Troutman; to Andre Mathews and his lovely mother; to Commissioner John White for his marketing expertise; to Barry Crumbley, Savannah Williams and Lee Fudge for having free spirits and sharing it with others; to Julia Rose Sampson, Keith Richards, Jean Mills, and John Rickel at SSAWG; to Errol R. Bragg and Jennifer-Claire V. Klotz at USDA Agricultural Marketing Services Wholesale & Alternative Markets; to Assistant Commissioner Public Affairs Division Brenda James Griffin of the Department of Agriculture State of Georgia and her lovely assistant Teresa Jenkins; to Georgia Commissioner of Labor Michael Thurmond; to Supreme Court of Georgia Chief Justice Robert Benham and Justice Carol Hunstein; to Yvonne J. Wiltz and members of the Atlanta Metropolitan Coalition of 100 Black Women; to Solicitor Carmen Smith and Georgia Association of Black Women Attorneys; to Anne Pritchard and staff at the State YMCA; to Hilton Young UGA Alumni Association; to Randy Demarco of Rose Printing; to Mrs. Frankie Phillips, Jay Funderburke of the Miller County Chamber of Commerce; to Cindy Awry who gave me a big boost with her contacts; to Marjean Boyd, Charlotte Phillips and Tammy Richardson, my hometown newspaper owners Mr. & Mrs. Terry Toole; to the Eastern Stars and their shining light; to Grand Worthy Matron Belle S. Clark and the Grand Master Benjamin Barksdale; to USDA employees, Ron Brown, Mary M. Parker, and Art Greenberg; to Patrick McElory of EverythingBlack.com; to George Howell; to the librarians at the East Point Public Library; to Nancy Saunders for praying for me; to Reverend Walter Kimbrough and the Cascade United Methodist Church for spiritual growth; to Pastor and Mrs. Brian Brooks of New Community Covenant Church for their support; to Jane Berry and Shauna Pennyman my writing partner; to Laura Whitfield; to my good friend Gary Love;to Roberta Bush, Gwen and Thaddeus Hodge; to my nieces and nephews who missed their aunt during the many days spent writing this book and to my ancestors who endured so much to make my life better.

TO ORDER BOOKS

✳✳✳

☎ Telephone orders: Call (404) 763-2536. Have your VISA
MasterCard or Amex ready

✳ On-line orders: EXPECTSUNSHINEBOOKS.COM
b-bush@BellSouth.com

✉ Postal orders: Museum Charity Publishing,
P. O. Box 90698
Atlanta, GA 30364

Please send the following books:_____

I understand that I may return any un-used books for a full refund

Name:_____

Address:_____

City:_____State:_____Zip_____

Telephone: (___) _____

Sales tax: Please add 7% for books shipped to Georgia addresses.

Shipping: **Price:**
$3.00 for each 1 book. $23.95 per book
Payment:
___ Check ____Money order
___ Credit card: ——VISA ——MasterCard

card number:_____

Name on card:_____Exp. date:____/___

Total: _____